L. T. Mea

The Girl and her Fortune

L. T. Meade

The Girl and her Fortune

1st Edition | ISBN: 978-3-75241-759-3

Place of Publication: Frankfurt am Main, Germany

Year of Publication: 2020

Outlook Verlag GmbH, Germany.

Reproduction of the original.

L.T. Meade
"The Girl and her Fortune"

Chapter One.

Leaving School.

Mrs. L. T. MEADE.

Brenda and Florence had both finished their school life. No pains had been spared to render them up to date in every particular. They had gone through the usual curriculum of a girl's education. Brenda was a little cleverer than Florence and had perhaps dived deeper into the heart of things, but Florence was the prettier of the two.

Now the last day of school was over. The last good-byes had been said. The last teacher had whispered words of affection in Brenda's ear, and the last and most loved school-fellow had kissed Florence on her pretty cheek and had hoped in that vague way which meant nothing at all that they should meet again. School belonged to the past. They had the world before them.

Florence was eighteen years of age, Brenda nineteen. To all intents and purposes they were children. Nevertheless, they regarded themselves as full-fledged women.

They were expecting an interview any day with their lawyer, Mr Timmins. Mr Timmins had provided the funds necessary for their education. He had arranged everything for them since the time when Florence at thirteen and Brenda at fourteen had lost their father and mother. Since then they depended on Mr Timmins—that is, as far as pounds, shillings and pence was concerned. He had seen them, not very often, but at intervals. He had always been nice and fussy and good, and had begged them to work hard. He had said to them over and over, "Be sure you don't miss your chance," and they invariably replied in the affirmative, and had assured him that they had no intention of missing it.

They had grieved for their parents, but that grief was now over. They were accustomed to the fact that they were fatherless and motherless. They had their dreams of the future, as most girls have. But the rough ways of the world had never hitherto assailed them.

In the holidays they always went to stay with a certain Mrs Fortescue. She was no relation; in fact, they were quite without relations. They were not only orphans, but they were relationless. The only children of an only son and an only daughter, they were solitary in the world, but that fact did not trouble them. They had never taken to their hearts the old proverb, that "blood is thicker than water." They were happy, healthy, everyday girls.

Florence was pretty, Brenda clever. They were really well-educated. Florence could sing very nicely—that is, for a girl of eighteen years of age. Her voice had possibilities which could even rise to a marketable value, but no one thought of the Heathcotes as people who required to make money by their accomplishments. They were supposed to be quite well off. They dressed well, the school they went to was expensive, and Mrs Fortescue charged quite a good sum for them in the holidays.

Mrs Fortescue was quite ordinary, but a lady. She knew nice people, and she introduced her young friends to them. The girls were welcomed by Mrs Fortescue's friends as desirable and even pleasant acquaintances. Mrs Fortescue took them out a little, and in her heart of hearts she thought of herself as their chaperone until they married. Of course they would marry. When their school-days were over, Mr Timmins, who arranged all their money matters, would take a house for them in London; and who so suitable to chaperone these nice, well brought up girls as Mrs Fortescue? She intended to suggest this to Mr Timmins when she saw him after their school work was over.

It had been arranged all along that they were to leave school when Florence was eighteen and Brenda nineteen. Some people said it was rather young, and that Florence ought to have an extra year of training in her special department. But then, when one came to consider it, she had no special department, she was good all round—that is, fairly good. Brenda was different. Brenda had real talent—well, perhaps that was the wrong word, but a real bias towards philosophy. She liked to read books on ethical subjects. She was fond of the works of Tyndale, Huxley, and Darwin. Sometimes she startled her acquaintances and friends by her ideas, all borrowed, of course, from these great writers. Nevertheless, even Brenda was not in the least remarkable, and as she was much plainer than Florence, it was the younger sister who was looked at, who was smiled at, who was approved of.

Well, the last day at school was over, and, as usual, the Misses Heathcote arrived at Mrs Fortescue's house at Langdale.

Langdale was a pretty town situated not very far from Tunbridge Wells. It was winter when the girls left school, and the snow was lying as a pure and beautiful mantle all over the fields when they drove up to Sunny Side, as Mrs Fortescue called her somewhat unpretentious house in the suburbs of Langdale. She came out to meet the girls and spoke to them with her usual affection.

"Ah, here you are!" she cried, "and welcome, welcome as flowers in May. You must be frozen, both of you. I have desired Jane to light a fire in your room; it is burning quite brightly. Come in, come in, my loves. I have been suffering a good deal from neuralgia, so won't go out into the porch. Higgins, take the young ladies' trunks round to the back entrance, where Bridget will attend to them."

The well-known cabman of the district said he would, and the girls found themselves shut into a warm hall, where a fire was lighted in the grate and where the place looked as homelike as it always did when they came back to it. They both kissed Mrs Fortescue as in duty bound. They liked her without loving her. She had never done anything for them except for a money consideration, and they knew this fact, although they did not speak of it. Somehow it seemed to keep their hearts at arm's length from her.

She was a pretty little woman of about forty years of age, with a keen, very keen eye to the main chance. Her own means were small. She was always glad to have the Heathcotes to help her to pay her Christmas bills and to enable her to take her summer holidays free. She looked upon them now as her property, and she always spoke of her house as their home.

The girls went up to their room. There Bridget, the one servant, who had served Mrs Fortescue for so long, was waiting for them. The room looked very pretty. There were two little beds side by side, ornamented with pink draperies at the back of the brass bedsteads, pink draperies at the foot, pretty pink eiderdowns covering the beds themselves, a nice green felt carpet on the floor, and green art serge window curtains, which were drawn now to keep out the wintry blast. The fire crackled and roared merrily. The room was sweet and fresh and clean. It had the fragrant smell of lavender. Mrs Fortescue grew a lot of lavender in her garden, and kept bags of it profusely sprinkled through her linen. The girls always associated the smell of lavender with Mrs Fortescue.

Bridget welcomed them back as she had done three times a year for so long now. They seemed never to remember anything else.

"How are you, Bridget?" said Florence, in her bright voice. "As well as ever, I hope?"

"Oh, yes, miss; what should ail me?" said Bridget.

She showed her teeth as she laughed, and looked gleesome and good tempered and pleasant. She felt as though she would like to kiss her two young ladies, as she invariably called the Misses Heathcote.

"Here is your hot water, miss," she said, turning to Brenda; "and I think the fire is all right, and dinner will be ready in ten minutes. If you want

6

anything else, you can ring for me."

She knew all about their trunks. There were invariably three trunks, two of which were kept in the storeroom downstairs, one of which came upstairs and was for immediate use. This trunk contained the girls' pretty blouses and ribbons, their sponge-bags, their night-cases, their brushes and combs, their slippers for use in the bedroom, and their pretty embroidered shoes to wear at dinnertime. Bridget had already unfastened this trunk. She glanced round the room just as she had done three times a year for the last four or five years, and then went away, leaving the young ladies to themselves. They were her young ladies; of course they would always come to Sunny Side. As far as she was concerned, this was only one more home coming, just like all the rest.

The girls hastily changed and made themselves smart, as was their wont, for dinner. Mrs Fortescue wanted them to look smart. She hated dowdy people. She always dressed extremely well herself, following the fashion as far as lay within her means, powdering her face, and arranging her dyed hair to the best possible advantage. She imagined that she did not look more than thirty years of age, but the girls knew quite well that her hair was dyed and her face powdered. They did not like her any the less for that, however. If she chose to be so silly, it was no affair of theirs. She was a good old thing. That is what they said to each other when they spoke of her at all—quite good-natured, and kind to them.

But Florence brushed out her radiant hair now with a kind of viciousness which she had never exhibited before, and as she coiled it round her stately young head, she turned and spoke to her sister.

"Do you like that new shade of Mrs Fortescue's hair or do you not, Brenda?"

"I did not notice it," said Brenda.

"Well, I did; and I think it is hideous. What blouse will you put on, Brenda?"

"I don't know: that pink one; won't that do?"

"No, it doesn't suit you. Wear white; I am going to."

Both sisters put on white blouses made in the extreme of the fashion. Florence's hair was one of her great beauties. It was of a very rich golden brown. She had quantities of it, and it had the natural fussiness and inclination to wave which made artificial means of producing that

7

result unnecessary. Brenda's hair was of a pale brown, without any wave or curl, but it was soft and thick and glossy. Brenda's eyes were exactly the same colour as her hair, and she had rather pale eyebrows. Her face was quite a nice little one, but not beautiful. Florence's face was beautiful—that is, it was beautiful at times. It could flash with animation, and her eyes could express scorn. She had a changing colour, too, and full red lips which revealed pearly teeth. Her looks were decidedly above the average, and there was a mocking light in her eyes which repelled and captivated at the same time.

Arm in arm, the two sisters went downstairs to the cosy drawing-room, where Mrs Fortescue was waiting for them.

"Ah, that is right, my loves. It is nice to see you both. Now I think I am entitled to a kiss, am I not?"

Florence went straight up at once and kissed the good lady on her forehead. Brenda did likewise.

"Aren't you hungry?" said Mrs Fortescue.

"Yes," said Brenda, "I am starving."

"And so am I," said Florence.

"Dinner is quite ready. Shall we all go into the dining-room?"

They went, the two fresh girls and the woman with the dyed hair, who imagined herself just as young as they—or rather tried to imagine herself their equal with regard to age. Mrs Fortescue looked at them with approval. She fancied she saw great success both for herself and Florence in Florence's face. Of course Florence would make a brilliant match. Some one would fall in love with her—if possible, some one with a title. Brenda must be content with a humbler fate, but she, too, would secure a mate. When Florence was not by, she was an exceedingly nice-looking girl, so placid and gentle and clever-looking. Mrs Fortescue was very proud of Brenda's cleverness. She liked to draw her out to talk on philosophical subjects. It was quite wonderful to hear her; and then that little tone—not of unbelief, oh no; but doubt, yes, doubt—was quite exciting and charming.

Brenda could talk better than Florence. The clergyman of the parish, Mr Russell, was unmarried. He would be an excellent husband for Brenda, just the very man, who would begin by converting her to truly orthodox views, and then would assure her how deeply he loved her. She would settle down at Langdale as the rector's wife. It would be an excellent position and very nice for Mrs Fortescue, who, of course, would be always dear Brenda's right hand, her mainstay in any perplexity. She knew that the rector's wife would hold an excellent position in a small town like Langdale. She would be the first lady in the place. To her would be given the task of leading what society there was to lead. She would have to discern the sheep from the goats. Those who were not admitted within the charmed circle would not be worth knowing.

Mrs Fortescue thought of all these things as she looked at Brenda across the dinner-table.

Presently, Florence laughed.

"What is the matter, dear?" said Mrs Fortescue.

"It seems quite incomprehensible," said Florence.

"What, my love? What do you mean?"

"Why, that our school-days are over. Things seem so exactly like they have always seemed. This is two days before Christmas. To-morrow we will go as usual to help with the church decorations. The next day will be Christmas Day. Then I suppose there'll be some sort of festivities going, and—and— But what I want to know is this?"

"Yes?" said Mrs Fortescue.

Bridget had left the room. An excellent dessert was on the board. The fire glowed red; the light was good.

"Yes?" she repeated.

"I want to know what is the end of it all. We are not going back to school at the end of January. We have done with school."

"Yes, darling," said Mrs Fortescue.

She rose as she spoke. She went swiftly up to the girl and put her arm round her neck.

"You have done with school in one sense, but all your beautiful future lies before you. You forget that Mr Timmins is coming to-morrow."

"I had forgotten," said Florence. "Had you, Brenda?"

"No," said Brenda, "how could I forget? I had a letter from him at Chester House this morning."

"What time did he say he would come, dear?" asked Mrs Fortescue.

"He said he would be here in the morning and he wanted us both to be in."

"He wants to talk to you about your future, darlings," said Mrs Fortescue; "very natural, very right. You had no idea, had you, Brenda, of going to Newnham or Girton I do trust and hope you had no thoughts in that direction. Men don't like women who have led collegiate lives: I know that for a fact; my own dear Frank often said so. He said he could not bear really learned women."

"I should have thought," said Brenda, "that men preferred women who could think. But I am afraid," she added, "that I don't very much care what men think on the subject. All the same, I am not going to either Newnham or Girton, so you can make your mind easy on that score, Mrs Fortescue."

"That is right, darling, that is right. I haven't an idea what Mr Timmins particularly wants to say to you, but I trust whatever he does say will be confided to me."

"Why, of course," said Florence.

"And in your future, darlings, I hope that I, your old friend, will bear a part."

The girls were silent, looking at her intently. She had expected an eager rush of words from those young lips, and their silence made her uneasy.

"I have done all I can for you, haven't I, my sweet ones?"

"Oh yes! You have been very kind, Mrs Fortescue," said Brenda.

"But that is not all," said Mrs Fortescue, her voice dropping. "I—and you must know it—I love you both."

Florence's fine dark eyes were opened to their fullest extent. Brenda looked very gently at the little woman with the dyed hair. Neither said a word. Mrs Fortescue sprang to her feet.

"We will go into the drawing-room now," she said. "You will tell me when you are sleepy and want to go to bed; would you like a game of cut-throat bridge first?"

The girls said they would like a game of bridge, and cards were produced. They played for about an hour, Mrs Fortescue invariably holding the best hand and the girls laughing good-humouredly at her luck. They played for love, not money. Mrs Fortescue thought the game uninteresting.

It was between ten and eleven when the sisters went up to their room. They said good-night to Mrs Fortescue on the landing.

They reached the comfortable bedroom where they had slept during the holidays for so many long years, and looked around them.

Florence suddenly said—

"Brenda, what should I do without you!" and Brenda flew to Florence, flung her arms round her neck and burst into tears.

"Why, what is it?" said the younger and taller sister of the two.

"I don't know," said Brenda.

She stopped crying almost immediately, mopped her eyes and smiled. Then she said, abruptly—

"I don't think I like Mrs Fortescue."

"That is wrong of you, Brenda. She has always been good to us."

"I know it is wrong of me," said Brenda, "not to like her, but all the same, I don't. I was never sure about it till to-night. Now I am practically certain I don't like her."

"But why?" said Florence. "Is it because she dyes her hair?"

"That is one thing," said Brenda. "The character of the woman who dyes her hair must be objectionable to me. I don't want her to have anything to do with my future. I shall tell Mr Timmins so to-morrow."

"Oh, will you really? She will be so terribly disappointed."

"I can't help it," said Brenda.

Florence had seated herself in a very comfortable easy-chair and Brenda was kneeling at her feet.

"You see," she said solemnly, "we have only one life in this world—one life and one youth, and I don't want mine to be commonplace. I think Mrs Fortescue would make it so. I can stand her for four weeks at Christmas; I can even endure her for seven weeks in the summer. But always! No, Flo, no: I couldn't endure her always, could you?"

"Oh," said Florence with a laugh, "I mean to get married very soon and have done with her. She will be quite useful until I am married. Why—how shocked you look, Brenda!"

"You are only eighteen; how can you think of such a thing as getting married?" said Brenda.

11

Florence laughed and stroked her sister's hair.

"I think of it very often," she said, "almost every day; in fact, it is the only thing before me. I mean to marry a rich and great man."

"But you must love him," said Brenda.

"I dare say I shall be able to manage that too," cried Florence.

Chapter Two.

A Startling Announcement.

The next day Mr Timmins arrived. He came by the train which reached Langdale at three o'clock. He invariably did come by that train. There was nothing at all remarkable in his paying the girls a visit. He was their business man. It was his custom to have an interview with them and with Mrs Fortescue at least once a year. It is true he had come last to see them in the summer, so that it was somewhat remarkable for him to state his intention of coming to Langdale again so soon. But the girls thought nothing at all about this, and if Mrs Fortescue did, she was more pleased than otherwise. Of course, now that her dear young charges had left school for ever, there would be a good deal to talk over and their future to be arranged. She would probably have to take a larger house. The cottage where she lived was very nice and quite sufficiently good to receive schoolgirls in the holidays; but it was not a fit home for young heiresses, who would naturally want to entertain company when they were at home, and who would also naturally require to visit the great world.

Mrs Fortescue felt excited. There were two years yet of her lease to run; but she thought she might manage to induce her landlord to take the little house off her hands, or she might sublet it. In all probability Mr Timmins would require her to live in London with the Misses Heathcote. He would himself choose a pretty house for her there. Her eyes shone as she thought of her future. In London she would have to dress better. She would, in all probability, have to visit one of those celebrated beauty shops in Bond Street in order to get herself quite up to the mark. There were all kinds of inventions now for defying the ravages of age, for keeping a youthful bloom on the cheek and a youthful lustre on the hair. It would be necessary for Mrs Fortescue to look as charming as ever in order to take her young charges about. How pleasant it would be to go with them from one gay assembly to another, to watch their innocent triumphs!

As she lay down in bed on the first night after their arrival she appraised with a great deal of discernment their manifest charms. Florence was, of course, the beauty, but Brenda had a quiet distinction of her own. Her face was full of intellect. Her eyes full of resource. She was dignified, too, more so than Florence, who was all sparkling and gay, as befitted the roses in her cheeks and the flashes of light in her big brown eyes. Altogether, they were a charming pair, and when dressed as they ought to be (how Mrs Fortescue would love that part of her duty!) would do anybody credit.

Mrs Fortescue and the Misses Heathcote! She could hear their names being announced on the threshold of more than one notable reception room, could see the eager light in manly eyes and the deference which would be shown to her as the chaperone of the young heiresses!

Yes, Mr Timmins' visit was decidedly welcome. He should have the very best of receptions.

On the day when Mr Timmins had elected to come it was Christmas Eve. In consequence, the trains were a little out of order, and Mrs Fortescue could not tell exactly when he would arrive.

"He said three o'clock, dears," she remarked to her young charges as they sat together at breakfast, the girls wearing pretty brown dresses which suited their clear complexions to a nicety. "Now, as a rule, the three o'clock train is in to the moment, but of course to-day it may be late—in all probability it will be late. I shall order hot cakes for tea; Bridget is quite celebrated for her hot cakes. We will have tea ready for him when he comes. Then when he has had his chat with me, he will want to say a word or two to you, Brenda, and you, Florence. You had better not be out of the way."

"We thought of going for a good walk," said Florence. "It is you, after all, he wants to see, Mrs Fortescue. He never has had much to say to us, has he?" Here she looked at her sister.

"No," said Brenda, thoughtfully. "But," she added, "when he wrote to me this time, he said he particularly wanted to see you and me alone, Flo. He didn't even mention your name, Mrs Fortescue."

"Ah well, dear," said Mrs Fortescue, with a smile; "that is quite natural. You have left school, you know."

"I can't quite believe it, can you, Brenda?" said Florence. "It seems just as if we must be going back to the dear old place."

"Oh, I don't know," said Brenda. "We are not going back: we said good-bye to every one, don't you remember?"

"You are never going back, dears, and for my part, I am glad," said Mrs Fortescue. "You will be my charge in future; at least, I hope so."

The girls were silent, looking hard at her. "As I have taken care of you since you were quite young girls, you will naturally wish for my protection until you are both married."

Brenda was silent. Florence said eagerly—"I mean to marry as soon as possible." Here she laughed, showing her pearly teeth, and a flashing light of anticipated triumph coming into her eyes.

"Of course you will marry soon, Florence," said Mrs Fortescue. "You are far too pretty not to be somebody's darling before long. And you, Brenda, also have an exceedingly attractive face. What are your dreams for the future, my love?"

"I cannot tell you," said Brenda.

She got up as she spoke, and walked to the window. After a time, she said something to her sister, and the girls left the room arm-in-arm.

Mrs Fortescue felt rather annoyed by their manners. They were very independent, as independent as though they were of age; whereas at the present moment they had not a shilling—no, not a shilling in the world that she did not supply to them under Mr Timmins' directions. Were they going to prove troublesome? She sincerely hoped not. They were good girls but that house in London might not be quite so agreeable as her dreams had pictured if Brenda developed a very strong will of her own and Florence was determined to marry for the sake of marrying. Still, Mr Timmins would put all right, and he would be with them at three o'clock.

The girls absented themselves during the whole of the morning, but appeared again in time for lunch, which they ate with a healthy appetite. They praised Mrs Fortescue's food, comparing it with what they had at school to the disadvantage of the latter. Mrs Fortescue was pleased. She prided herself very much on Bridget's cooking.

"And now," she said, when the meal had come to an end, "you will go upstairs and put on your prettiest dresses and wait in the drawing-room for Mr Timmins. I shall not be far off. He will naturally want to see me as soon as he has had his talk with you both, so I shall remain writing letters in the dining-room. There are so many letters and cards to send off at Christmas time that I shall be fully occupied, and when you touch the bell, Brenda, I shall know what it means. In any case, I will send tea into the drawing-room at a quarter to four. That will give you time to get through your business first, and if you want me to come in and pour out the tea, I shall know if you will just touch the bell."

"Thank you," said Brenda. "But it isn't half-past one yet, and the day is a lovely one. Florence and I want to take a good brisk walk between now and three o'clock. We shall be back before three. We cannot be mewed up in the house until Mr Timmins chooses to arrive."

"Oh, my dear children! He will think it queer."

"I am sorry," said Brenda, "but he had no right to choose Christmas Eve as the day when he was to come to see us. His train may not be in till late. Anyhow, we want to take advantage of the sunshine. Come, Florence."

The girls left the room and soon afterwards were seen going out arm-in-arm. They walked down the little avenue, and were lost to view.

There was a certain style about them both. They looked quite different from the ordinary Langdale girls. Florence held herself very well, and although she acknowledged herself to be a beauty, had no self-conscious airs. Brenda's sweet face appeared to see beyond the ordinary line of vision, as though she were always communing with thoughts deeper and more rare than those given to most. People turned and looked at the girls as they walked up the little High Street. Most people knew them, and were interested in them. They were the very charming young ladies who always spent their holidays with Mrs Fortescue. They were, of course, to be included in all the Christmas parties given at Langdale, and Mrs Fortescue would, as her custom was, give a party on Twelfth Night in their honour.

That was the usual state of things. The girls did not seem in the mood, however, to greet their old friends beyond smiling and nodding to them. As they were returning home, Brenda said—

"We are more than half an hour late. I wonder if he has come."

"Well, if he has, it is all right," said Florence. "Mrs Fortescue is dying to have a chat with him all by herself, and she will have managed to by this time. She will be rather glad, if the truth may be known, that we are not in to interrupt her. I can see that she is dying with curiosity."

"I don't want her to live with us in the future," said Brenda.

"But she has set her heart on it," said Florence.

"I know," remarked Brenda; "but, all the same, our lives are our own, and I don't think we can do with Mrs Fortescue. I suppose Mr Timmins will tell us what he has decided. We are not of age yet, either of us. You have three years to wait, Flo, and I have two."

"Well, we must do what he wishes," said Florence. "I intend to be married ages and ages before I am twenty-one; so that will be all right."

While they were coming towards the house, an impatient, white-headed old lawyer was pacing up and down Mrs Fortescue's narrow drawing-room. Mrs Fortescue was sitting with him and doing her utmost to soothe his impatience.

"Dear Mr Timmins, I am so sorry the girls are out. I quite thought they would have been back before now."

"But they knew my train would be in by three o'clock," said Mr Timmins.

He was a man of between fifty and sixty years of age, rather small, with rosy cheeks and irascible eyes. His hair was abundant and snow-white, white as milk.

"I said three o'clock," he repeated.

"Yes," said Mrs Fortescue, "but on Christmas Eve we made sure your train would be late."

The lawyer took out his watch.

"Not the special from London; that is never late," he remarked. "I want to catch the half-past four back; otherwise I shall have to go by one of those dreadful slow trains, and there's a good deal to talk over. I do think it is a little careless of those girls not to be at home when they are expecting me."

Mrs Fortescue coughed, then she 'hemmed.

"It might—" she began. The lawyer paused in his impatient walk and stared at her. "It might expedite matters," she continued, "if you were to tell me some of your plans. For instance, I shall quite understand if you wish me to leave here and take a house in London. It is true the lease of this house won't be up for two years, but I have no doubt my landlord would be open to a consideration."

"Eh? What is it you were going to say? I don't want you to leave your house," blurted out Mr Timmins. "I have nothing whatever to do with your future, Mrs Fortescue. You have been kind to my young friends in the past, but I think I have—er—er—fully repaid you. And here they come—that is all right. Now, my dear madam, if you would leave the young ladies with me—no tea, thank you; I haven't time for any—I may be able to get my business through in three-quarters of an hour. It is only just half-past three. If I leave here at a quarter-past four, I may catch the express back to town. Would you be so very kind as to order your servant to have a cab at the door for me at a quarter-past four—yes, in three-quarters of an hour I can say all that need be said. No tea, I beg of you."

He was really very cross; it was the girls' doing. Mrs Fortescue felt thoroughly annoyed. She went into the hall to meet Brenda and Florence.

"Mr Timmins has been here for nearly twenty minutes. His train was in sharp at three. He is very much annoyed at your both being out. Go to him at once, girls—at once."

"Oh, of course we will," said Florence. "Who would have supposed that his train would have been punctual to-day! Come, Brenda, come."

They went, just as they were, into the pretty little precise drawing-room, where a fire was burning cheerily in the grate, and the room was looking spick and span, everything dusted and in perfect order, and some pretty vases full of fresh flowers adding a picturesqueness to the scene. It was quite a dear little drawing-room, and when the two girls—Florence with that rich colour which so specially characterised her, and Brenda a little paler but very sweet-looking—entered the room, the picture was complete. The old lawyer lost his sense of irritation. He came forward with both hands outstretched.

"My dear children," he said; "my poor children. Sit down; sit down."

They were surprised at his address, and Florence began to apologise for being late; but Brenda made no remark, only her face turned pale.

"I may as well out with it at once," said Mr Timmins. "It was never my wish that it should have been kept from you all these years, but I only obeyed your parent's special instructions. You have left school—"

"Oh yes," said Florence; "and I am glad. What are we to do in the future, Daddy Timmins?"

She often called him by that name. He took her soft young hand and stroked it. There was a husky note in his voice. He found it difficult to speak. After a minute or two, he said abruptly—

"Now, children, I will just tell you the very worst at once. You haven't a solid, solitary hundred pounds between you in this wide world. I kept you at school as long as I could. There is not enough money to pay for another term's schooling, but there is enough to pay Mrs Fortescue for your Christmas holidays, and there will be a few pounds over to put into each of your pockets. The little money your father left you will then be quite exhausted."

"I don't understand," said Brenda, after a long time.

Florence was silent—she, who was generally the noisy one. She was gazing straight before her out into Mrs Fortescue's little garden which had a light covering of snow over the flower-beds, and which looked so pretty and yet so small and confined. She looked beyond the garden at the line of the horizon, which showed clear against the frosty air. There would be a hard frost to-night. Christmas Day would come in with its old-fashioned splendour. She had imagined all sorts of things about this special time; Christmas Day in hot countries, Christmas Day in large country houses, Christmas Day in her own home, when she had won the man who would love her, not only for her beauty, but her wealth. She was penniless. It seemed very queer. It seemed to contract her world. She could not understand it.

Brenda, who had a stronger nature, began to perceive the position more quickly.

"Please," she said—and her young voice had no tremble in it—"please tell me exactly what this means and why—why we were neither of us told until now?"

Mr Timmins shrugged his shoulders.

"How old were you, Brenda, when your father and mother died?" he asked.

"I was fourteen," she answered, "and Florence was thirteen."

"Precisely; you were two little girls: you were relationless."

"So I have always been told," said Brenda.

"Your father left a will behind him. He always appeared to you to be a rich man, did he not?"

"I suppose so," said Brenda. "I never thought about it."

"Nor did I," said Florence, speaking for the first time.

"Well, he was not rich. He lived up to his income. He earned a considerable amount as a writer."

"I was very proud of him," said Brenda.

"When he died," continued Mr Timmins, taking no notice of this remark —"you know your mother died first—but when he died he left a will, giving explicit directions that all his debts were to be paid in full. There were not many, but there were some. The remainder of the money was to be spent on the education of you two girls. I assure you, my dears, there was not much; but I have brought the accounts with me for you to see the exact amount realisable from his estate and precisely how I spent it. I found Mrs Fortescue willing to give you a home in the holidays, and I arranged with her that you were to go to her for so much a week. I chose, by your father's directions, the very best possible school to send you to, a school where you would only meet with ladies, and where you would be educated as thoroughly as possible. You were to stay on at school and with Mrs Fortescue until the last hundred pounds of your money was reached. Then you were to be told the truth: that you were to face the world. After your fees for your last term's schooling have been met and Mrs Fortescue has been paid for your Christmas holidays, there will be precisely eighty pounds in the bank to your credit. That money I think you ought to save for a nest-egg. That is all you possess. Your father's idea was that you would live more happily and work more contentedly if you were allowed to grow up to the period of adolescence without knowing the cares and sorrows of the world. He may have been wrong; doubtless he was; anyhow, there was nothing whatever for me to do but to obey the will. I came down myself to tell you. You will have the Christmas holidays in which to prepare yourselves for the battle of life. You can tell Mrs Fortescue or not, as you please. She has learned nothing from me. I think that is about all, except—"

"Yes?" said Florence, speaking for the first time—"except what?"

"Except that I would like you both—yes, both—to see Lady Marian Dixie, a very old client of mine, who was a friend of your mother's, and I believe, would give you advice, and perhaps help you to find situations. Lady Marian is in London, and if you wish it, I will arrange that you shall have an interview with her. What day would suit you both?"

"Any day," said Brenda.

Florence was silent.

"Here is a five-pound note between you. It is your own money—five pounds out of your remaining eighty pounds. Be very careful of it. I will endeavour to see Lady Marian on Monday, and will write to you. Ah, there is my cab. You can tell Mrs Fortescue or not, just as you please. Good-bye now, my dears, good-bye. I am truly sorry, truly sorry; but those who work for their own living are not the most unhappy people, and you are well-educated; your poor father saw to that. Don't blame the dead, Brenda. Florence, think kindly of the dead."

Chapter Three.

Plans for the Future.

Mrs Fortescue was full of curiosity.

The girls were absolutely silent. She talked with animation of their usually gay programme for Christmas. The Blundells and the Arbuthnots and the Aylmers had all invited them to Christmas parties. Of course they would go. They were to dine with the Arbuthnots on the following evening. She hoped the girls had pretty dresses.

"There will be quite a big party," said Mrs Fortescue. "Major Reid and his son are also to be there. Michael Reid is a remarkably clever man. What sort of dresses have you, girls? Those white ones you wore last summer must be rather *outré* now. It was such a pity that I was not able to get you some really stylish frocks from Madame Aidée in town."

"Our white frocks will do very well indeed," said Florence.

"But you have grown, dear; you have grown up now," said Mrs Fortescue. "Oh my love!" She drew her chair a little closer to the young girl as she spoke. "I wonder what Mr Timmins meant. He did not seem at all interested in my house. I expressed so plainly my willingness to give it up and to take a house in town where we could be all happy together; but he was very huffy and disagreeable. It was a sad pity that you didn't stay in for him. It put him out. I never knew that Mr Timmins was such an irascible old gentleman before."

"He is not; he is a perfect dear," said Florence.

"Well, Florence, I assure you he was not at all a dear to me. Still, if he made himself agreeable to you, you two darling young creatures, I must not mind. I suppose I shan't see a great deal of you in the future. I shall miss you, my loves."

Tears came into the little woman's eyes. They were genuine tears, of sorrow for herself but also of affection for the girls. She would, of course, like to make money by them, but she also regarded them as belonging to her. She had known them for so long, and, notwithstanding the fact that she had been paid for their support, she had been really good to them. She had given them of those things which money cannot buy, had sat up with Florence night after night when she was ill with the measles, and had read herself hoarse in order to keep that difficult young lady in bed when she wanted to be up and playing about.

Of the two girls Florence was her darling. She dreamed much of Florence's future, of the husband she would win, of the position she would attain, and of the advantage which she, Mrs Fortescue, would derive from her young friends—advancement in the social scale. Beauty was better than talent; and Florence, as well as being an heiress, was also a beauty.

It cannot be said that the girls did much justice to Bridget's hot cakes. They were both a little stunned, and their one desire was to get away to their own bedroom to talk over their changed circumstances, and decide on what course of action they would pursue with regard to Mrs Fortescue. In her heart of hearts, Florence would have liked to rush to the good lady and say impulsively—

"I am a cheat, an impostor. I haven't a penny in the world. You will be paid up to the end of the Christmas holidays, and then you will never see me any more. I have got to provide my own living somehow. I suppose I'll manage best as a nursery governess; but I don't know anything really well."

Brenda, however, would not encourage any such lawless action.

"We won't say a word about it," said Brenda, "until after Christmas Day."

She gave forth this mandate when the girls were in their room preparing for dinner.

"Oh," said Florence; "it will kill me to keep it a secret for so long!"

"It won't kill you," replied Brenda, "for you will have me to talk it over with."

"But she'll go on asking us questions," said Florence. "She will want to know where we are going after the holidays; if we are going to stay on with her, or what is to happen; and unless we tell her a lot of lies, I don't see how we are to escape telling her the truth. It is all dreadful from first to last; but I think having to keep it a secret from Mrs Fortescue is about the most terrible part of all."

"It is the part you feel most at the present time," said Brenda. "It is a merciful dispensation that we cannot realise everything that is happening just at the moment it happens. It is only by degrees that we get to realise the full extent of our calamities."

"I suppose it is a calamity," said Florence, opening her bright eyes very wide. "Somehow, at the present moment I don't feel anything at all about it except rather excited; and there are eighty pounds left. Eighty pounds ought to go far, oughtn't they? Oughtn't they to go far, Brenda?"

"No," said Brenda; "they won't go far at all."

"But I can't make out why. We could go into small lodgings and live quite by ourselves and lead the simple life. There is so much written now about the simple life. I have read many books lately in which very clever men say that we eat far too much, and that, after all, what we really need is abundance of fresh air and so many hours for sleep and very plain food. I was reading a book not long ago which described a man who had exactly twenty pounds on which he intended to live for a whole year. He paid two and sixpence a week for his room and about as much more for his food, and he was very healthy and very happy. Now, if we did the same sort of thing, we could live both of us quite comfortably for two years on our eighty pounds."

"And then," said Brenda, "what would happen at the end of that time?"

"Oh, I should be married by then," said Florence, "and you would come and live with me, of course, you old darling."

"No; that I wouldn't," said Brenda. "I am not at all content to sit down and wait. I want to do something. As far as I am concerned, I am rather glad of this chance. I never did care for what are so-called 'society pleasures.' I see now the reason why I always felt driven to work very hard. You know father was a great writer. I shall write too. I will make money by my books, and we will both live together and be happy. If you find your prince, the man you have made up your mind to marry, why, you shall marry him. But if you don't, I am always there. We will be very careful of our money, and I will write a book; I think I just know how. I am not father's daughter for nothing. The book will be a success, and I shall get an order for another book, and we can live somehow. We shall be twenty thousand times happier than if we were in a house with Mrs Fortescue looking out for husbands for us—for that is what it comes to when all is said and done."

"Oh, you darling! I never thought of that," said Florence. "It is perfectly splendid! I never admired you in all my life as I admire you now, Brenda. Of course, I never thought that you would be the one to save us from destruction. I used at times to have a sort of idea within me that perhaps you would have to come and live with me some day when all our money was spent. I can't imagine why I used to think so often about all our money being spent; but I used to, only I imagined it would be after I had got my trousseau and was married to my dear lord, or duke, or marquis—anyhow, some one with a big place and a title; and I used to imagine you living with me and being my dear companion. But this is much, much better than any of those things."

"Yes; I think it is better," said Brenda. "I will think about the book to-night, and perhaps the title may come to me; but in the meantime, we are not to tell Mrs Fortescue—not at least till Christmas Day is over; and we've got to take out our white dresses and get them ironed, and see that they look as fresh as possible. Now, we mustn't stay too long in our room: she is dying with curiosity, but she can't possibly guess the truth."

"No; she couldn't guess the truth, that would be beyond her power," said Florence. "The truth is horrible, and yet delightful. We are our own mistresses, aren't we, Brenda?"

"As far as the eighty pounds go," replied Brenda.

"What I was so terrified about," said the younger sister, "was this. I thought we should have to go as governesses or companions, or something of that sort, in big houses and be—be parted." Her lips trembled.

"Oh no; we won't be parted," said Brenda; "but all the same, we'll have to go to see Lady Marian Dixie—that is, when she writes to ask us. Now may I brush your hair for you? I want you to look your very prettiest self to-night."

The white frocks were ironed by Bridget's skilful fingers. It is true, they were only the sort of dresses worn by schoolgirls, but they were quite pretty, and of the very best material. They were somewhat short for the two tall girls, and Brenda smiled at herself when she saw her dress, which only reached a trifle below her ankles. As to Florence, she skipped about the room in hers. She was in wonderfully high spirits. For girls who had been brought up as heiresses, and who expected all the world to bow before them, this was extraordinary. And now it was borne in upon her that she had only forty pounds in the world, not even quite that, for already a little of the five pounds advanced by Mr Timmins had been spent. Mrs Fortescue insisted upon it. She said, "You ought to wear real flowers; I will order some for you at the florist's round the corner."

Now flowers at Christmas time are expensive, but Florence was reckless and ordered roses and lilies of the valley. Brenda looked unutterable things, but after opening her lips as though to speak, decided to remain silent. Why should not Florence have her pretty way for once? She looked at her sister with great admiration. She thought again of her beauty, which was of the sort which can scarcely be described, and deals more with expression than feature. Wherever this girl went, her bright eyes did their own work. They drew people towards them as towards a magnet. Her charming manners effected the rest of the fascination. She was not self-conscious either, so that women liked her as much as men did.

But now Christmas Day had really come, and Mrs Fortescue, in the highest of high spirits, accompanied her young charges to Colonel Arbuthnot's house. Year by year, the girls had eaten their Christmas dinner at the old Colonel's house, which was known by the commonplace name of The Grange. It was a corner house in Langdale, abutting straight on to the street, but evidently at one time there had been a big garden in front, and just before the hall door was an enormous oak tree, which spread its shadows over the low stone steps in summer, and caused the dining-room windows which faced the street to be cool even in the hottest weather.

At the back of the house was a glorious old garden. No one had touched that. It measured nearly three acres. It had its walled-in enclosure, its small paddock, and its wealth of flower garden. The flowers, as far as Florence and Brenda could make out, seemed to grow without expense or trouble, for Colonel Arbuthnot was not a rich man, and could not even afford a gardener every day, but he worked a good deal himself, and was helped by his daughter Susie, a buxom, rather matronly young woman of six or seven and thirty. The girls liked Susie very much, although they considered her quite an old maid.

No; Colonel Arbuthnot was by no means rich—that is, as far as money is concerned; but he possessed other riches—the riches of a brave and noble heart. He was straight as a die in all his dealings with his fellow-men. He had a good deal of penetration of character, and had long ago taken a fancy to Mrs Fortescue's young charges. It did not matter in the least to him whether the girls were heiresses or not. They were young. They were both, in his opinion, pretty. He liked young and pretty creatures, and the idea of sitting down to his Christmas dinner without these additions to his party would have annoyed him very much.

Colonel Arbuthnot's one extravagance in the year was his Christmas dinner. He invited all those people to it who otherwise might have to do without roast beef and plum pudding. There were a good many such in the little town of Langdale. It was a remote place, far from the world, and no one was wealthy there. Money went far in a little place of the sort, and the Colonel always saved several pounds out of his income in order to give Susie plenty of money to pay for a great joint at the butcher's, and to make the old-fashioned plum pudding, also to prepare the mince pies by the old receipt, and to wind up by a sumptuous dessert.

It was on these rare occasions that the people who came to The Grange saw the magnificent silver which Colonel Arbuthnot possessed. It was kept wrapped up in paper and baize during the remainder of the year: for Susie said frankly that she could not keep it clean; what with the garden and helping the young servant, she had no time for polishing silver. Accordingly, she just kept out a few silver spoons and forks for family use and locked the rest up.

But Christmas Day was a great occasion. Christmas Day saw the doors flung wide, and hospitality reigning supreme. The Colonel put on his best dinner coat. He had worn it on more than one auspicious occasion at more than one famous London club. But it never seemed to grow the least bit old-fashioned. He always put a sprig of holly with the berries on it in his button-hole, and would not change this symbol of Christmas for any flower that could be presented to him.

As to Susie, she also had one dinner dress which appeared on these auspicious occasions, and only then. It was made of a sort of grey "barège," and had belonged to her mother. It had been altered to fit her somewhat abundant proportions, and it was lined with silk. That was what Susie admired so much about it. The extravagance of silk lining gave her, as she expressed it, "a sense of aristocracy." She said she felt much more like a lady with a silk lining in her dress than if she wore a silk dress itself with a cotton lining.

"There is something pompous and ostentatious about the latter," she said, "whereas the former shows a true lady."

She constantly moved about the room in order that the rustle of the silk might be heard, and occasionally, in a fit of absence—or apparent absence—she would lift the skirt so as to show the silk lining. The dress itself was exceedingly simple; but that did not matter at all to Susie. She wore it low in the neck and short in the sleeves; and it is true that she sometimes rather shivered with cold; for on no other day in the remaining three hundred and sixty-four did she dream of putting on a low dress. In the front of the dress she wore her mother's diamond brooch—a treasure from the past, which alone she felt gave her distinction; and round her neck she had a string of old pearls, somewhat yellow with age, but very genuine and very good.

Susie's hair was turning slightly grey and was somewhat thin, but then she never remembered her hair at all, nor her honest, flushed, reddish face, hardened by exposure to all sorts of weather, but very healthy withal.

From the moment she entered the drawing-room to receive her guests, she never gave Susie Arbuthnot a thought, except in the very rare moments when she rustled her grey barège in order to let her visitors know that the lining was silk. That silk lining was her one vanity. As a rule, we all have one, and that was hers. It was a very innocent one, and did no one any harm.

On this special Christmas Day, the Reids were coming to dinner. Major Reid was an army man who had retired a long time ago. He was always expecting his promotion, but had not got it yet. He was somewhat discontented, but liked to talk over old days with Colonel Arbuthnot. His son Michael had been a favourite with the Heathcote girls as long as they could remember. He was considered to be of their own rank in life, and Mrs Fortescue, in consequence, asked him to dine, and play with them during the holidays. When he was very small, he rather bullied them; but as he grew older, he began to think a great deal of Florence's beauty, and even to imagine himself in love with her. He was the sort of young man who always kept his father in a state of alarm with regard to money, and spent a great deal more than he had a right to do. He was a good-looking fellow, and popular in his regiment; and as he could make himself very agreeable, was a great favourite.

When Christmas Day dawned on the snowy world, Major Reid spoke to his son.

"Well, Michael," he said, "it's a great pleasure to have you with me. I consider myself a particularly lucky fellow to be able to say that I haven't missed a single Christmas since your birth without having you by my side. But I don't suppose this state of things will go on. You are sure to accept foreign service between now and next year, and, all things considered, I should like you to marry, my boy."

"Oh, I'm a great deal too young for that kind of thing," said Michael, helping himself to some kidneys on toast as he spoke, and eating with great relish and appetite.

"Well, my boy, I don't know about that, there's nothing like taking time by the forelock. Why, how old are you, Mike?"

"I shall be twenty-four my next birthday," said the young man.

"Well," said the major; "many a man has married before then, and done none the worse."

"And a great many have ruined their lives by marrying too young," said Reid. "Besides, I am only a lieutenant, father; I ought not to think of such a thing until I get my captaincy."

Major Reid looked attentively at his son.

"The fact is, Michael," he said, "you ought to marry money. Of course, to engage yourself to a girl who has not plenty of money would be sheer madness."

Michael Reid looked at his father with a twinkle in his grey eye. He had quite a nice face, although it was very worldly. He could read through the old man's thoughts at the present moment as though they were spread before him on an open page.

"What are you thinking of, dad?" he said. "Out with it, whatever it is."

"This," said the Major, colouring as he spoke; "those two girls have come back to Mrs Fortescue's. Florence is remarkably pretty. They must both be exceedingly well off. I spoke to Mrs Fortescue the other day, and she told me that she doesn't know the extent of their fortune, but believes it to be something quite considerable. In fact, I should imagine from the way they have been brought up, that they must have something which runs into at least four figures a year. Now, the moment such girls go into society, they will be surrounded by adventurers, men who wish to secure them simply for the sake of their money. You, my dear boy, I understand, have already paid attentions to Florence, and why not carry them on? This is your chance; she is an exceedingly attractive girl: in fact, she is a beauty. She will be rich. At present you are not supposed to know anything about her fortune; but if it comes as a surprise, why, so much the better."

Lieutenant Reid, of His Majesty's —th, thought of certain debts he had incurred, debts which if he explained their full significance to his father, would ruin the old man. He sat silent for a time, thinking.

"When last I saw Florence," he said, after a minute's pause, "she was just a pretty little hoyden of a girl; but, as you say, we were always good friends. Did you say they were still with Mrs Fortescue?"

"Of course they are," said Major Reid, tapping his foot impatiently. "Don't they always spend their holidays with her? But they are leaving school now, in fact, they have left school. Mrs Fortescue quite expects to go to London with them in order to take them into the gay world. If ever you have a chance, it is now; and if I were you, I would make the best of it."

Michael Reid was silent, but he broke a piece of toast, and ate it reflectively. His father saw that he need say no more, and after a minute's pause left the room.

As to the young man, he went to church on that Christmas Day although he had no previous idea of doing so. He did not dare even to say to himself that his object was to see the Misses Heathcote. But he looked very hard at both girls as they walked up the aisle of the church, accompanied by Mrs Fortescue. Even in her plain school dress, Florence had an air of distinction, and Brenda looked quiet and charming. Michael Reid felt his heart beating quite agreeably. His father's advice, after all, was sound. If he could secure a wife who had four, five, six, or seven hundred a year—and, of course, there was a great likelihood that she would have much more—why, his fortune would be made. Florence had seen no other man as yet, but she had a schoolgirl friendship for him. Now was his opportunity. He would strike while the iron was hot.

Accordingly, in the course of the afternoon, as he and his father were pacing up and down in the sheltered corner by the laurel hedge beside the Major's old house, Michael linked his hand within the old man's arm, and said—

"If you will allow me to manage things my own way, and will not appear in the very least to interfere; why—I—I will do my best."

"Thank you, my boy. I knew you would," said the Major. "God bless you, my son; and God grant you success."

Michael did not think it necessary to reply to these remarks, which were really uttered as a matter of course; but he went upstairs early to his bedroom, and took great care in selecting the white tie he would wear with his dinner suit that evening. Instead of the morsel of mistletoe, which was considered the correct thing among the young ladies at Langdale for the gentlemen to wear at the Arbuthnots' dinner parties, he went out and purchased a rose. He paid a shilling for a rose with a bud attached, and put it with care into his button-hole. When he had finished dressing, he surveyed himself in the glass with great satisfaction. He was a good-looking fellow, and might, he thought, attract the admiration and affection of any girl. He tried hard to remember what colour Florence's eyes were; but hers was an evasive face, which baffled inquiry. It was full of subtle changes. The eyes looked brown one moment, green the next; and then again a careful observer would swear that they were grey. But they had a story in them at all times. So Michael thought to himself. He thought that to compare them to the stars of heaven would be a happy metaphor, and that he might use it with effect that evening. He hoped the night would be fine, so that they could go out between the dances. They always danced at Colonel Arbuthnot's on Christmas night. When dinner was cleared away, the tables were pushed to one side, and the polished floor left ready for the tread of the dancers.

Then was Susie's really proud moment. She would sit at the old piano —never in perfect tune—and play one old-fashioned waltz and old-fashioned polka after another. She played a set of the Lancers too when she was pressed to do so; but was often heard to say she considered them too rompy. Notwithstanding, she was never tired of rattling out her old tunes on the old piano; and Reid thought of the dancing and of the happy minute when he would get Florence to himself under the stars and compare her bright eyes to those luminaries.

When he had finished dressing, he went downstairs and spoke to his father.

"You are going in a cab, I suppose, as usual?"

"Well, yes; there's a good deal of snow on the ground, and it is some little distance to the Arbuthnots', so I told Hoggs to call. Dinner is at seven. The cab will be here at ten minutes to the hour."

"You don't greatly mind if I walk on in advance?"

"Of course not, my boy, if you prefer it. But be sure you put on good stout walking shoes, and change them for your pumps when you get in."

"All right, Dad," said this soldier of his Majesty's —th Foot; and, slipping on an overcoat, he stepped out into the frosty night.

Yes; the stars at least would be propitious. Although there were great banks of cloud coming up from the west, they were moving slowly, and he did not think they would interfere with the enjoyment of that Christmas dinner.

Lieutenant Reid was the very first of the guests to arrive at the Arbuthnots' house. In fact, he was so much too early that the little maid who was hired for the occasion had not her cap on, and kept him waiting at the hall door for a considerable time. But at last he was admitted, and was ushered into the Colonel's smoking-room, that apartment being set aside for the accommodation of the gentleman guests. There Reid changed his walking shoes for his pumps, took off his overcoat, looked at his face in the glass, saw that his button-hole was in perfect order, and was the very first to enter the drawing-room.

There he saw to his immense satisfaction Susie Arbuthnot standing by the fire quite alone. The Colonel had not yet come downstairs. Susie, in that grey barège, with a flush of excitement all over her face, Susie with her very stout figure, her diamond brooch, her pearl necklace, gave Reid an extraordinary desire to laugh. While all the world was going on, poor Susie was standing still. It flashed through his mind after a minute's reflection that when he and Florence were married, they would send her anonymously a fashionable new dinner dress. He began to consider what colour it ought to be—purple, mauve, red, violet? He decided to leave the choice of the dress to Florence, who, of course, would know all about such things. Meanwhile, he went eagerly up to shake hands with the little lady.

"You are early, Captain," she said.

She invariably called him "Captain," and although he had no right whatever to the name, he enjoyed the sound very much, and never dreamed of correcting her.

"I do hope," she continued, her brow puckering slightly, "that nothing has occurred to keep your dear, good father from joining in our Christmas festivities. I don't know what the Colonel would say if the Major were not present at our Christmas dinner. Do tell me at once, Captain, that nothing is wrong with your esteemed father."

"Nothing whatever," said Reid; "he is coming along presently in one of Hoggs' cabs. I thought I would come first for the simple reason that I want to have a word alone with you, Miss Susie."

"Oh, I am only too delighted," said Susie; and she rustled her silk petticoat as she spoke, getting closer to the young man, and looking redder in the face than ever. "What is it? If there is anything in my power—"

"Oh, it is quite a simple matter," he said. "You know I dine out a great deal, but I may say without verging a hair's line from the truth, that I never enjoy any dinners as I do yours—a little old-fashioned of course —but so good, the food so—A.1. Now I noticed last Christmas that you, Miss Susie—ah! Miss Susie!—you must have been in London since I saw you last and picked up some of the modes of the great world. I noticed that you had adopted some of the latest London fashions: for instance, the names of the guests put beside their plates."

"It was Lady Lorrimer, when she was here two years ago, who told me about that," said Susie. "I generally use a number of correspondence cards, cutting them very carefully to the necessary shape, and printing the names in my very best writing. It helps our servants, and our visitors know where to sit."

"Quite so. I think it is an excellent idea. But please tell me—where am I to sit at dinner to-night?"

She laughed, and half blushed. She had meant this good "Captain Reid" to take herself in to dinner, having reserved a much more elderly lady for Major Reid. But somehow, as she looked into his face, an intuition came to her. She was a woman with very quick intuitions, and she could read a man's thoughts in a flash.

"Never mind whom you were to take in," she said. "Tell me quickly— quickly—whom you wish to sit next. Ah, there's another ring at the bell!"

"Well, to tell you the truth, I want to take Florence Heathcote into dinner to-night. Can you manage it?"

"I certainly can, and will. Dear, beautiful Florence! No wonder you admire her. I will give directions this minute. Just sit down, won't you, near the fire. I will go and alter the dinner-table."

Lieutenant Reid seated himself with a smile round his lips. He had achieved his purpose.

"I thought she would help me," was his inward reflection. "I was to take her in—poor Susie! but I am flying for higher game. 'Pon my word! the pater is right, and Florence is worth making an effort to secure. Now, it's all right. We'll go into the garden after dinner, and during dinner I can begin to lay my little trap for the entanglement of that gentle heart. She looked very beautiful in church to-day, but I do wish I could remember the colour of her eyes."

Chapter Four.

Christmas Festivities.

At night there was no doubt whatever that Florence Heathcote's eyes looked their best. By night they were invariably dark; their brightness was enhanced by artificial light. They were softened, too, particularly at such a table as Colonel Arbuthnot and his daughter prepared for their guests. For nothing would induce the Colonel to have anything but candles on his dinner-table. Candles, in large silver branches, adorned the board; and if girls don't know, they ought to be informed that there is no possible light so soft and becoming to eyes and complexion as that caused by these minor stars of illumination. There is no garishness in the light of a candle, and it does not make hideous revelations like electricity nor cause the deep shadows that a gaselier flings on your head.

Florence, in spite of herself, was feeling a little sad to-night, and that sadness gave the final touch to her charms. She was quite pleased to be taken into dinner by her old playmate, Michael Reid. She told him so in her sweet, bright, open way.

"What a lot we shall have to talk of!" she said. "How long is it since I have first known you?"

He tried to count the years on his fingers and then, moved by an inspiration, said—

"No; I won't count—I can't count. I have known you for ever."

"Oh," she said, with a laugh; "but of course you haven't." And then, rather to his horror, she called across the table to Brenda—"When did we first meet Michael? I mean, how old were you?"

Brenda was talking very gently to an elderly clergyman—a dull sort of man, who always, however, appealed to Brenda because, as she said to her sister, he was so very good. She paused and looked thoughtful; and Susie, at the bottom of the table, gave her silk lining a swish. After a minute's thought, Brenda said—

"We have known you, Michael, for four years." And then she related in a gentle but penetrating voice the occasion of their first meeting. "Florence was," she said, "fourteen at the time. She is eighteen now. You pulled her hair: you were a very rough boy indeed, and you made

Flo cry."

"No, that he didn't!" interrupted Florence. "He put me into a towering passion."

"Yes," pursued Brenda, "and you cried while you were in the passion."

"I don't know how to apologise," said the somewhat discomfited lieutenant: "but I suppose boys will be boys."

"And girls will be girls," said Florence. "You would not pull my hair now, would you?"

He looked at her lovely hair, arranged in the most becoming fashion and yet so simply, and murmured something which she could not quite catch but which caused her ears to tingle, for she was quite unaccustomed to compliments except among her school-fellows, and they did not count.

After dinner, the pair found themselves alone for a few minutes. Then Reid drew a chair close to Florence's side, and said—

"I wish with all my heart and soul that you were as poor as a church mouse, so that I might show you what a man's devotion can do for a girl."

Florence found herself turning pale—not at the latter part of his speech but at the beginning; for was she not quite as poor as a church mouse? in fact, poorer, for even the church mouse manages to exist; and she could not exist beyond quite a limited time on the small amount of money which the girls possessed between them.

By and by the dance began, and they did go out under the stars. Reid felt almost in love. He had always admired pretty Florence, and to-night she looked so charming—so young, so very girlish, and yet there was a certain stateliness about her. She was an unopened bud as yet, but full of rare promise. He thought of what she might be in a year—in two years. Other men would discover her charms. Oh, if only she would promise herself to him!

He did not dare to say too much that night; but while he was thinking about her, and she was looking up at the stars, and his chance of making that remark about her eyes was so very easy, she suddenly said something which put the whole idea out of his head.

"You have made a remarkable statement since we came here this evening, and I do just wonder if you meant it."

"I meant every single word I said. How could I possibly mean anything else to you?"

"That is what I want to find out. I am very young, and you are the only man I have ever known. At school we used to talk about men and what they did and said and thought; and, of course, we always had our dreams."

"Of course you had," said Reid. "All girls have. Do whisper to me what yours were like."

"No; I can't do that, for they were so fleeting. One day I imagined one thing about a man, another day, another. But you said the sort of thing to me to-night which—which I did not expect, and which—which I can't forget."

"Do tell me what it was," asked the puzzled lieutenant. He was racking his own brain to remember.

"You expressed a wish that I were as poor as a church mouse. What a very funny thing to say!"

"Oh, it's that you are thinking of," said Reid. "Well, I meant it. I meant that I should like you to be poor in order to show you what a fellow will do for a really lovely girl whom he—" and then he drew himself up abruptly and said no more, for he was afraid of going too far.

"Thank you," said Florence. "Then you are one of the men who do not care for a girl because she is rich?"

"I!" said Reid, being certain by Florence's manner that she must have over a thousand a year. "I should hate myself if I did."

"I am so glad to hear it," said Florence. "I respect you very much."

"I am glad—" he said, in a gentle tone.

"Do let us walk up and down by the laurel hedge; we needn't go in for the next dance, need we?"

"I promised it to Mr Cunliffe."

"Oh—cut his dance. Never mind him; stay with me. Surely I am more interesting to you than Cunliffe."

"Yes, you are; far more interesting: in fact, I don't care about him at all. Nevertheless, I don't like to cut men's dances."

"You will have plenty of opportunity to make up for all omissions when you go to London. I suppose you will be going there soon."

"Perhaps so," said Florence; who, however, by no means wished to revert to her future.

"When you go," pursued Lieutenant Reid, "you will see plenty of me, for I am quartered at Knightsbridge for the present. I shall come to see you whenever I can."

"That will be very kind of you."

"Not at all. It is not a kindness to give oneself a pleasure—at least, I don't think so."

Florence made no reply. After a time she said, suddenly—

"I *am* glad you made that remark. I shall never forget it—never."

Again he had to ask her what it was.

"About your feeling just the same to me if I were as poor as a church mouse."

"So I should," he answered, with enthusiasm. "How could riches enhance your value? A man likes a girl for herself. He is indifferent, quite indifferent as to whether she has money or not."

"That is the sort of man I admire," said Florence.

"Well, always remember that I have said it of you. Don't forget, will you?"

"I shall never forget," she replied; and then they went back to the house where Susie, being tired out with strumming on the old piano, had begged for round games. There was a great deal of fun; and altogether Christmas night passed with *éclat*. The girls went back in high spirits, and as they were going to bed that evening, Florence said to Brenda—

"How did you enjoy yourself?"

"Fairly well," she replied; "but I saw that you looked happy."

"I was," said Florence. "I have found one true man in the world."

"Michael Reid?" remarked Brenda. "You talked and danced with him a good deal."

"Yes; he said one queer thing—in fact, he said it three times. He must be a very good fellow, better even than—than we imagined."

"What did he say?" asked Brenda, as she unfastened her sister's white frock, and slightly yawned, for she was tired and wanted to go to bed.

"He said that he would like a girl quite as well if she were as poor as a church mouse. He said it so earnestly, too. He knows nothing about us, but you know that sort of remark would not have been believed by the girls at school; would it, Brenda?"

"No; I expect not. Well, you are as poor as a church mouse, Flo, but you didn't tell him so?"

"Of course I didn't. No one must know before poor Mrs Fortescue, and I suppose she must be told after we have been to London to see Lady Marian Dixie. All the same, Brenda, I can't realise it a bit. Things are going on just as usual, and we are to stay here till the end of our holidays. We have till at least the twentieth of January to be happy in. Why should we be miserable till then?"

"I have no intention of being miserable," was Brenda's remark.

A few minutes later, the girls got into bed and slept with that sound refreshing sleep which only comes to most of us in early youth. The next day, Lieutenant Reid did himself the pleasure of calling on Mrs Fortescue. He said he came to see her, but he looked decidedly disappointed when he was told that both the girls were out.

"They are with Susie Arbuthnot," she said. "They went early this morning and won't be back until late. I think they are going to have tea at the Arbuthnots'." Mr Reid's face decidedly fell. "But you and I will have tea together," said Mrs Fortescue; "and I can tell you about the dear girls. I can see that you are much interested in them."

"Can you?" he asked, looking at her critically.

She laughed.

"Of course I can," she said. "Why, you hardly left my beautiful Florence's side the whole of yesterday evening. You ought not to pay such marked attentions if you don't mean anything by them."

"But suppose I do mean something," he said, all of a sudden.

Then Mrs Fortescue drew her chair nearer to that of the gallant lieutenant and spoke with great earnestness.

"I have not the least idea," she said, "what the girls' fortunes will be; but I know, of course, that they must be exceedingly well off. No expense has been spared during their school-days. Their dress has been quiet but of the most expensive make, and they have been taught every possible accomplishment, even riding, which you know is always a serious item in school bills. Mr Timmins is a very reserved man, and has told me nothing of what is now to happen to them."

"But surely, you must know something?" said the lieutenant, who at that moment seemed quite to forget that he would like Florence equally well if she were as poor as a church mouse.

"As a matter of fact, I know nothing. Mr Timmins came down to see the girls on Christmas Eve, and was with them for a little time, but he had no talk with me. Still, I make not the slightest doubt that I shall hear from him soon and, in all probability, we shall leave Langdale and go to London. I am quite willing to go with the dear children and to help them any way in my power."

"They will both marry young," said the lieutenant, with exceeding gloom in his voice. "They will be surrounded by suitors of all sorts. A homely sort of fellow like—like—"

"Oh, you mustn't compare yourself to a homely sort of fellow," said Mrs Fortescue.

"An officer in His Majesty's army! A soldier can take his place with any man."

"I know; but then I have nothing of my own, nothing at all, except what my dear old father allows me. I ought not to think about the girls—about either of them."

Mrs Fortescue paused to consider.

"I don't know that you ought," she said. She had her own ideas for her young charges, and Lieutenant Reid, a native of Langdale, would bring no special credit to her management. People would say that it was a pretty romance; the girl and the young man met when they were still children. But that was all they could say about a young and beautiful heiress marrying a penniless man. After a pause, she said—

"You have not really confided in me, and, of course, if there is true and passionate and real love, I am the last person to stand in the way; but without it I think both those young girls ought to have their chances."

Mrs Fortescue spoke with precision and reserve. Reid thought her a tiresome woman, and hoped sincerely that some one else would chaperone the girls when they first went to London. His intention, however, was to secure Florence before that date. He thought he had already made an impression on her, and if Mrs Fortescue did not help him, Susie Arbuthnot would. Susie was the very soul of romance. Behind Susie's red face shone a soul, the kindest and most chivalrous in the world; and Susie's true heart beat for all that she considered true in love and bravery. A man must be brave, and a man must be loving.

That was all she considered necessary, and surely Lieutenant Reid, the young man she had known from a boy, possessed these two attributes. Yes, he would give up Mrs Fortescue, and consult Susie on the subject of Florence Heathcote.

Accordingly, he declined tea, although some special hot cakes were being made for him in the kitchen, and went away holding his head very high and looking, as Mrs Fortescue said to herself, "quite distinguished."

"I must be careful not to allow my dear Florence to see too much of him," she said to herself. "It would never do for her to fall in love with him before she has seen other men."

Reid strolled about in the neighbourhood of the Arbuthnots' house until, as it were quite by accident, he came across the merry girls and equally merry Miss Arbuthnot returning home from their walk. They were carrying sprays of holly and quantities of mistletoe, and looked each one of them, in her own way, quite charming. Reid fell naturally to Florence's share, and Brenda and Susie walked on in front.

When they got to the front door, Susie invited "dear Captain Reid" to come in and have tea with them, and dear Captain Reid accepted the invitation with alacrity.

"It is so funny," said Florence, "to hear her invariably call you 'Captain': and you never correct her; why don't you?"

"Because I like the sound," he answered. "I shall be Captain, I hope, before long; and I like it, for your sake."

"For my sake?" she said, colouring faintly.

"Yes; there is nothing I would not do for you. There is no ambition that would not fill my heart and soul for your sake. You know that, Florence, don't you?"

"I don't," said Florence, rather bluntly. "I can't imagine for a single moment why you talk as you do."

"I only felt that you must know," he answered. He was a little piqued by her manner; but then, when he looked into her eyes—yes, they were dark grey to-day, and he did admire dark grey eyes, they were so expressive—he felt that she, herself, alone, independent of thousands, was a girl worth winning. He really began to be quite in love with her. He delighted in the feeling which she gave him. He wondered if it was really true, and if he would be steadfast to her if she were as poor as a church mouse. But then he thought again with a throb of delight how unnecessary that feeling was, for Florence would be rich; only he must secure her before she went to London.

Tea was brought in, and the tea was excellent. There were several nice cakes and choice little dainties left after the dinner of the day before, and Colonel Arbuthnot joined the social gathering and made himself extremely agreeable, and in the end Reid accompanied the young ladies back to Mrs Fortescue's house.

With Brenda by his side, he could not say anything special to Florence, but it was already quite perceptible that he liked her and had singled her out for attention. Susie Arbuthnot noticed it; so did the Colonel; and so certainly also did Mrs Fortescue.

Mrs Fortescue was the only one who was annoyed. The Reids were a good old family. Michael Reid, as far as any one knew, had always been an excellent fellow. He had done well at school, and had passed into the Army with ease. There was no reason why he should not marry a girl with money, particularly as he liked her.

So said Colonel Arbuthnot, who knew nothing about the young fellow's debts. Susie, who had been talking the matter over with her father, quite started and coloured a somewhat ugly red when Major Reid was announced.

Major Reid sat down in the chair which his son had just occupied, and immediately began to talk about the Heathcote girls.

"How different they are from others," he said. "I have seldom seen any one quite—to my ideas—so beautiful as Florence."

Then Colonel Arbuthnot said something which made Susie long to wear her grey barège in order that she might rustle the silk. He said gravely—

"Your son seems to agree with you, Major."

"Ah!" said the Major. "Do you think so? Well, nothing could give me greater happiness."

After that Susie got up to leave the room, but her father called her back.

"We have no secrets from you, Tabby," he said.

Tabby was his favourite name for her, and she sat down again near his side.

"The fact is," said the Major, "I want Mike to settle down, and I don't believe that anything will do him real good, or bring out the best that is in him, like marriage. I think that Florence Heathcote would make him an admirable wife. Of course, he could not afford to marry without money, but as she has plenty, that would make no difficulty. I think, too, he would care for her for herself."

"Oh, I know he would; he loves her dearly?" said romantic Susie. "Now that you have spoken, I will tell you a little incident. He came here on purpose last night, before any one else, in order to make sure that he was to take her in to dinner. I don't mind confessing to you, Major Reid, that I had arranged differently; but after he had spoken of it, there was no help for me. I made the change quite easily—"

"Good girl; good girl!" said the Major. "Well, if he asks me to give him my blessing on such a match, you may be quite sure I shall do so. But we must await events; things cannot be hurried; the girl is very young."

"She is indeed," said Colonel Arbuthnot; "nothing more than a child."

It was on the next day that the girls received a letter from Mr Timmins. It was addressed to Miss Heathcote, and was sealed with a large red seal. It had a thick and massive appearance, and caused Mrs Fortescue pangs of intense curiosity as she handled it before her young charges came downstairs to breakfast. There was no other letter that morning, so she was able to turn it round and look at the seal, which bore the inscription of "Timmins and Co, Solicitors, Chancery Lane," and also to feel the bulk of the epistle. It was a long envelope, and Mrs Fortescue felt absolutely devoured with curiosity with regard to the contents. To open, however, a sealed envelope was an impossibility, and she did not dare even to attempt the work.

She was seated quietly in front of her copper urn when the girls came in.

"Well, my dears," she said; "how are you? I hope you have slept well."

"Capitally, thank you," said Brenda; and then her eyes flew to her plate, and she saw the long letter lying on it. She turned a little pale, and a swift contraction went through her heart.

Florence, however, did not even glance at the letter. She danced into the room in her usually gay and sprightly manner and sat down, saying as she did so—

"Oh, I am so hungry. I do hope that we have something very nice for breakfast."

"You know I always think of your tastes, dears," said Mrs Fortescue, who felt more than ever inclined to pet the girls that morning. "I have got the most delicious kippers and that special porridge with cream which you like so much. There will be hot cakes afterwards, so I hope you will have enough to eat."

"Oh yes, yes!" said Florence. "Am I not hungry!"

She glanced at her sister as she spoke, and saw that Brenda's grave eyes were fixed on the letter. Brenda had not attempted to open it. She had laid it quietly by her plate.

"Who is your correspondent?" asked Florence.

"I don't know," said Brenda; "but I suppose it is from Mr Timmins."

Then Florence somehow felt her appetite going and a coldness stealing over her. But Mrs Fortescue was in the best of spirits.

"I am delighted the man has written," she said. "It was so queer of him to come down on Christmas Eve and have a long talk with you two girls and not say a word to me. Of course, you know, my darlings, that you are to me as my very own children, and there is nothing I would not do for you—"

"You would keep us with you if we were as poor as church mice, for instance," said Florence, raising her eyes (they looked brown this morning) and fixing them with a saucy air on the good lady's face.

"Indeed I would. I love you far beyond mere money. But what I want to say to you is this,"—Mrs Fortescue broke a piece of toast as she spoke, and her voice became a little nervous—"that whatever Mr Timmins intends to do for your future, I do trust he will not leave me out of it. I do not think it would be right of him, seeing that I have had the care of you ever since you have been both little children."

"We have been most of our time at school, have we not?" said Brenda.

"Yes, dear; that is quite true; but who has prepared you for your school, and who has done her utmost to make your holidays happy?"

"Indeed, you have!" said Brenda, her voice full of feeling. "You have been most kind."

"That is all I want you to say, Brenda. Well, what I wish is to go on being kind. You will probably go to London, and I should like to go with you. Until you marry, my dears—and alas! I fear that auspicious event will take place soon with you both,"—here she glanced at Florence, who grew quite red—"until you marry, you will need a chaperone, and who so suitable as me? If you see Mr Timmins, will you mention to him, dears, that I am more than anxious to do for you in the future what I did in the past?"

"Yes, oh yes; we will be sure to say it," said Florence in a glib tone.

Breakfast went on. Brenda did not attempt to open her letter.

"I wonder why you don't read what the good man has said," remarked Mrs Fortescue. "He probably, to judge from the size of that letter, has given you full directions with regard to your future plans. I cannot imagine why he does not write to me."

"I will read the letter, if you like," said Brenda in her gentlest voice.

"Do so, dear; I should be so much obliged."

Brenda opened it. There was a long foolscap sheet which, as far as Mrs Fortescue's acute vision could discern, was filled with accounts; and then there was a letter. The accounts pleased her, only she was puzzled that they had not been sent to her. Hitherto, she had always been consulted about the dear girls.

The letter was very short, and when Brenda had run her eyes over it, she folded it up and put it back into its envelope, placing the accounts also there for future study.

"Well, well?" said Mrs Fortescue, with great interest.

"Mr Timmins wants us both to go up to London to-morrow to see him."

"And, of course, I am to go with you."

"He does not say so; in fact, I know he wishes us to go alone."

"That is very odd."

"He tells us the train to go by," pursued Brenda, "and also the train by which we can return. If we leave here at nine o'clock to-morrow morning, we shall get to London a little before twelve. We can be back with you in time for dinner or supper."

"And he says nothing about my going?"

"He does. He says he wishes us to go alone; that we are to travel first-class. He sends us a postal order for our fares."

"First-class!" said Mrs Fortescue, with a sniff. "Of course girls in your position will travel first-class. It is absurd even to think of any other mode of travelling."

"Yes," said Brenda calmly, "he says first-class, and he has sent us the money."

"He wants to talk to you about your future, dears."

"Probably," said Brenda. "We shall have to go," she continued, and she looked across at Florence.

Florence said "Yes," but her tone was not very lively. Mrs Fortescue glanced at her.

"She is thinking of Lieutenant Reid," was her thought. "Poor child! Well, of course, he is handsome and well-born, and she has plenty of money, only I always did think that with her great beauty she would be the one to make the best match. However, there is no interfering with nature, and if she loves him—and beyond doubt he loves her—it will be all right." Aloud Mrs Fortescue said—

"You had better send a telegram to Mr Timmins to tell him you will go up by the train you mention. I will prepare sandwiches for you for the journey, and take you to the station and come again to meet the train by which you return. Nothing will induce me to neglect even a particle of my duty: you may be certain of that, my loves. Only I do hope, Brenda, that if you can put in a word for one who truly loves you, during your interview with Mr Timmins, you will mention me as the chaperone you would like best."

"I will mention you with real affection," said Brenda; and she got up as she spoke and, going up to the little woman, kissed her on her forehead. Then she said, gently: "Mr Timmins specially says not to send a telegram—that a postcard will do equally well."

Chapter Five.

A Proposal and a Promise.

Soon after lunch on that day Florence went out alone to execute some small commissions for Mrs Fortescue. She was wearing a sealskin cap and very *chic* little sealskin jacket. No one could look nicer than she did in her pretty and expensive dress, and nothing could become her radiant complexion and those changeful eyes of hers better than the sealskin cap, which revealed beneath its narrow brim just a touch of that bright chestnut hair which Lieutenant Reid thought of by day and dreamed of by night. It was only last night that he dreamed he was touching that hair and even kissing it and calling it his own. Now it was a queer dream, for his locks were harsh and, of course, very short, and although he had thick hair, it was not exactly beautiful. He could only have called Florence's chestnut locks his own in one sense. Somehow, as he lay in bed that morning and thought about the girl, he imagined himself more than ever in love with her.

"I do care for her, quite independently of her money," he thought. "She is the happiest, happiest girl on earth, and the most beautiful. I always had a *penchant* for her, but now I am in love with her."

In love. He smiled to himself at the thought. He had read a lot about that passion which sometimes destroys a man's life, and sometimes blesses it, but which, when it is strong and all-enduring, has a very great effect either for good or for evil.

Lieutenant Reid, as he luxuriously stretched himself in bed, thought it an agreeable feeling, and that those who talk about it exaggerate its importance a good deal. Of course he had had his fancies before now. He had liked to flirt like other men, but never, never before had he thought of any one as he thought of Florence. She was all that his fancy could desire—

A creature not too bright and good For human nature's daily food.

For daily pleasures, simple wiles.

Praise, blame, love, kisses, tears and smiles.

He was quite delighted with himself for remembering Wordsworth's ideal of the perfect woman, and said to himself that he must really be in love. He showed symptoms of the complaint that morning by not taking quite such a large breakfast as usual, and also by being strangely silent while Major Reid chatted on the invariable subjects which now interested him—those local matters which he as a magistrate of the peace was engaged in, viz the poachers in the neighbourhood, the state of the autumn crops, the distress amongst the poor, his own extremely light purse.

His remarks with regard to his purse did rouse Michael Reid's attention. There was not the slightest doubt that he would have to speak to his father about that five hundred pounds which he owed. It must be met somehow, and that before very long. He owed it to one man in particular, a money-lender, who had no pity and no idea of allowing the debt to lie over beyond the day when it was due. Exactly five hundred pounds would be expected to be paid to him in a month's time, therefore before that date he must be properly engaged to his darling Florence. He would then be absolutely a free man. Five hundred pounds was such a trifle. No young man in his position could exist in the Army without getting into debt. Florence need never know about it. His father would pay it gladly when once he knew that his son was securing over a thousand a year. Florence's income would probably be fifteen hundred a year at the least. If that was the case, he would pay his father back with interest during the first year of their marriage; and she, his darling Florence, need know nothing at all about it. It was not likely that a sharp old card, as he designated Mr Timmins, would allow Lieutenant Reid the full control of Florence's fortune. But her income—dear innocent child!—she would only too gladly put it into his hands to use as he thought best. Her tastes, sweet girl, were quite simple. No; he must not lose his chance—not that there was any special hurry, but still, before she went to London he must secure her. He was thinking of her, therefore, of her fortune, of that dreadful debt which was still, however, quite a month off as he walked down the High Street and suddenly met the pretty, radiant creature in her becoming sealskin cap and jacket, and muff to match.

She was all in brown to-day, for her dress was made of some brown stuff too, and her boots were brown, and very small and pretty. He liked a woman to have pretty feet, and beyond doubt Florence had. Altogether, she was, as he expressed it, admirably turned out. She was a charming young creature. His heart beat with the intoxication of first love as he drew close to her side. He took off his hat and came up to her eagerly.

"This is luck!" he said.

She coloured. She was really interested in him. A man who could care for a girl who was as poor as a church mouse must be worth something, and she had never before in her young experience met any young man—that is, on terms of equality. Major Reid's son had been indifferent to her as a boy, but as a man he was quite agreeable and—yes—very good-looking. So she, too, stopped, and expressed pleasure in her dancing brown eyes (yes, they were brown to-day; he thought, after all, he liked them when they were brown best) and said—

"I am glad I have met you. Are you going anywhere in particular?"

"I am going wherever you are going," he said, taking his cigarette from his mouth and throwing it away.

She laughed in a very soft and musical way. "If you go with me," she said, "you will have a very dull time. I am only out to do some shopping for Mrs Fortescue. She has given me a list of things to get from James, the grocer, and also, I am to buy a duck for dinner at Henderson's. You won't care to accompany me on these stupid expeditions."

"Oh yes, I shall," he answered. "I will stay outside while you go in and shop. I will be ever so patient. I know what a long time young ladies take shopping. But it won't matter to me; that is, if you give me my reward."

"What is that?" she asked, raising her dancing eyes, filing them on his face, and then looking down again and colouring faintly; for his bold black eyes had said something to hers which caused her heart to beat and which she did not in the least understand.

"Well," he said, "my reward is this. The day is lovely. Why won't you take a walk with me afterwards?"

"But I shall be late for lunch. Mrs Fortescue always has lunch ready at one o'clock."

"Never mind: if you are out she and Brenda will lunch alone. Do come with me, Florence, do. I want to talk to you so badly."

Florence remembered his speech about the church mouse. He did like her for herself. Of course he must not be told yet. No thought of her money had ever entered into his unworldly soul. He was nice. After all, why should she not have a bit of fun? It was tiresome walking with him in the presence of Susie Arbuthnot and Brenda. Why not walk with him all alone?

"I will go with you," she said, "if you will give me lunch somewhere. For when one o'clock comes, I shall be very hungry and will want something to eat."

"Then I tell you what we'll do," said the gallant lieutenant in a resolute tone, and thinking with great satisfaction that he had an unbroken sovereign in his pocket. "I will take you as far as Johnson's, by the river side; it is two miles from here, and we will have the very choicest little lunch I can possibly order, and have a good time by ourselves."

"But what will Mrs Fortescue think?" said Florence.

"You can send her a note, if you like. James would send it with the groceries."

"So he would—so he would!" said Florence. "Very well: I will go with you; it will be great fun!"

She skipped along by his side; it seemed impossible to her to walk like other girls; she was always upheld by a sort of inward spring which made her appear almost like a creature with wings. Her extreme youth and childishness were made more than ever apparent by the way she walked.

They reached the shop. Florence gave orders with regard to the groceries and scribbled a line to Brenda, telling her that she had met Michael Reid, and was going for a walk with him and would be back before dusk. The duck was also ordered for late dinner, and then the pair sped away into the country as fast as their legs could carry them. Florence said she liked to walk fast, and Michael agreed with her. He hated girls who were not strong: he hated delicacy of any sort. Florence was quite perfect. She had such magnificent health. He did not believe she even had the faintest idea what it was to be tired. Florence, with a smile, assured him that such was the case—she *did* not know; she was always well. Brenda, poor darling, sometimes had headaches, but she, Florence, never had.

"It is a good thing that I am strong, isn't it?" she said with a laugh.

He replied in the affirmative.

By and by they reached Johnson's, an inn by the river side, much frequented in the summer by all sorts and conditions of people, and in the winter carrying on a fair trade by bicyclists.

On this special day, however, the inn parlour was empty and the young pair had it to themselves. Reid felt more in love than ever as he showed the *menu* to Florence, and consulted with her over the special dainties they were to have for lunch. She said she would like beefsteak best and plenty of onions. She hoped he did not mind onions. He said he adored them, and Florence laughed and showed her white teeth.

She really was an adorable girl; and her tastes were so simple. He asked her what she would like to drink, and she said water. He ordered water, therefore, for her and a bottle of Guinness' stout for himself.

While they were partaking of their lunch, Florence told him that she and Brenda were going to London on the following day.

"We are going to see Mr Timmins," she said.

"Oh, your lawyer?" he remarked at once. "He is going to arrange with you about your future?"

"Yes," she replied, very gravely; and she looked him full in the face.

He returned her glance.

"You are not going to stay in London, are you?"

"Oh no," she answered. "Oh no; we are both going up by the nine o'clock train. We are travelling first-class."

"Why, of course," said Lieutenant Reid. "I only wish I might come with you."

"Oh no," said Florence, "you must not do that. He does not even wish poor Mrs Fortescue to come. He wants to see us quite alone."

"He is going to make arrangements about you; I quite understand," said the lieutenant.

It was there and then he made up his mind. If he did not seize the present opportunity, Florence, beautiful Florence would be snatched from him. Some one else, perhaps some horrid City magnate with lots of money, would come forward and win the darling girl. It could not, it must not be.

They had finished their lunch and the lieutenant had paid for it, gallantly giving a substantial tip to the red-elbowed girl who had waited on them. They then left the cottage and went slowly along by the river side.

The river was very full just now and made a babbling sound. The snow and cold of Christmas had given place to milder weather. There was quite a spring-like feel in the air, and the lieutenant felt more in love than ever.

"Florence," he said suddenly, "do you remember what I said to you on Christmas night?"

"You said a great many things to me then," she answered, somewhat flippantly; "I cannot remember them all."

"But there was one very special thing, and I think I said it several times."

"Oh, now I remember," she said colouring, and a different expression came into her face. Her eyes grew large and dark and were turned upon him with a certain solemnity, with a look as though she would read him through.

"Tell me, tell me with your own lips what I said," was his answer. He trembled as he spoke; he was feeling desperately in love.

"You said," answered Florence, "that you wished I was as poor as a church mouse in order that you could show me what—what you would do for me."

"And—and I repeat it now," he said.

He looked at her again. Her eyes filled with sudden tears.

"What is the matter, darling?" was his next remark. "Oh, Florence! I love you with all my heart and soul. I love you for yourself—absolutely and entirely. Say you will love me; do—do give me hope. Don't throw yourself away on some worthless fellow. Give me a chance, Florence."

Florence was a good deal startled. All girls have dreamt of their first proposal, and when the proposal comes it is generally as unlike their dreams as any one thing can be unlike another. But there was something about this one, coming as it did at this special time, which touched the girl inexpressibly.

"Will you give me," she said, "one month in which to consider the matter?"

He thought of his debt, that debt which must be met in a month's time. He could not keep his father in uncertainty until then.

"No," he said. "No; say now that you will marry me—now; promise me now, my own little Florence. If you care for me the least bit now, you will love me twice as well in a month's time."

"Give me a week then," she answered.

"I must think the matter over for a week—and say just once again to me that you would like me to be as poor as a church mouse in order to show me how much you care for me."

He was obliged to be satisfied with this, but he talked love to her all the way home, and before they reached the village of Langdale he had even kissed her once on her forehead. Oh yes; he was in love. All was right.

"Remember, in one week I come to you for the fulfilment of your promise, Florence," was his answer when at last they parted outside Mrs Fortescue's door.

Chapter Six.

At Mr Timmins' Office.

That evening late, Florence, in the seclusion of their chamber told Brenda what had happened.

"You know," she said, "that we have nothing. I think it is dreadful of Mr Timmins to make a mystery about it, and to let us appear before the good folks at Langdale as apparently wealthy girls; but on one matter, at least, I am obliged to him. This has given me the opportunity of finding a true heart."

"A true heart, Flo?" said Brenda. "What do you mean?"

"What I say," answered Florence. "You know I took a walk to-day with Michael Reid."

"Oh, with poor old Michael," said Brenda, in a tone as much as to say that Michael at least did not count for much, that he was a poor sort of fellow, and need not agitate the girls just then. But Florence's next words astonished her elder sister very much.

"I am a year younger than you," said Florence, "and I have been proposed for before you, Brenda. Michael cares for me; he cares for me for myself alone. He absolutely wants me to be poor, very poor, as poor as a church mouse, he says, in order that he may show to all the world how deeply he loves me. He doesn't care for me in the very least because he thinks I have money. He wants me to be poor: he told me all about it to-day. He mentioned the subject first at the Arbuthnots' Christmas party, but he spoke of it again to-day when we were walking home. He looked very, very handsome; and I—I quite think I like him."

"Oh, you poor little innocent Florence!" said Brenda. "But you don't know anything about men at all. It was very mean of him to speak to you, very mean of him to take advantage of you. Yes, it was, Flo; I cannot help saying it. It was wrong of him; he ought not to have done it."

"He did nothing wrong," said Florence; "he spoke up like a man. I suppose a man can't help loving a girl."

"He ought not to have done it like that," repeated Brenda. "I know I am right: he ought on no account to have done it like that."

"It is very queer of you to speak to me in that tone, Brenda," said her sister, "and I must say that I am very much astonished. I cannot understand what you mean. Why should not Michael care for me? He is a gentleman: he is an officer in the King's army. We know his father; we know his people. I don't know why you should talk to me like that. I suppose a man will propose to me some day, just as some one will propose to you, darling Brenda; and you will love him with all your heart and soul."

"Oh, I don't know," said Brenda. "I am not beautiful like you, Flo. But tell me all about it, darling. You startled me very much when you first spoke, and I suppose I did wrong to be a little bit annoyed. It hurts me to think that my only darling sister should care for any one else better than me."

"But I don't know that I do," said Florence; "only of course," she added, "he was very nice, and he did say so emphatically that he only cared for me for myself."

"And what did you say to him, Flo?"

"I told him that he had startled me, and that I wanted a month to think it over. He would not give me a month, but he gave me a week. What I feel is this, Brenda: that he must know all about our changed circumstances before I give him my true answer. Then if he comes forward, as indeed I know he will, I shall feel at least assured that he cares for me for myself."

"And who would not care for you for yourself," said her sister, putting her arms round the girl's neck and kissing her with great affection. "Why, aren't you just the dearest creature in the world? Won't you make the very sweetest wife? But all the same," she added, "I don't know how Mr Reid can marry any one at present, for he can't be well off. I know the Major has barely enough to live on."

"We should be very poor, of course," said Florence; "but he seems to like that. After all," she continued, "what I thought was this: that I might, if I go on liking him as much as I do now, be engaged to him, and we could wait a year or so while I—I was earning money. It does seem so queer to think that I should have to earn money in any way; and I am sure I haven't the faintest idea how to set about it—not the very faintest. But I suppose Mr Timmins will give us some sort of directions to-morrow."

"I suppose he will," said Brenda. "It is queer, the whole thing. We have been allowed to grow up, you and I, as though we were rich girls. We have had every possible luxury and every possible educational advantage, and I know the people at Langdale think us rich enough, and yet we haven't a penny in the world."

"Oh yes!" said Florence; "we have seventy-five pounds; don't forget that: that is quite a good sum—at least, it seems so to me."

"Half of it would buy your trousseau—at least some sort of trousseau for you, if you decide to marry the lieutenant at once," said Brenda. Then she added: "It is all very puzzling; but you must do what you think right; only we won't tell Mrs Fortescue anything whatever about it."

After this conversation, the girls went to bed, and both slept the sleep of the just, pretty Florence looking prettier than ever in her happy innocent dreams—for was she not loved just for her very self alone, and was not that something to be proud of?

They were awakened early in the morning by Mrs Fortescue, who herself brought them tea to their room, and fussed over them, and paid them a vast amount of attention, and begged of them, as they were getting ready for their journey, not to forget to put in a good word for her when Mr Timmins talked about their future plans. She was quite excited about them, and her cheeks were flushed, and her eyes had a hard, worried look. Brenda felt as though they were exceedingly deceitful to her, but Florence was thinking of Lieutenant Reid, and had not much time to consider Mrs Fortescue and her future.

A cab arrived in good time to take them to the station. Mrs Fortescue herself accompanied them to the train, and purchased their tickets for them out of the postal order which had been cashed the day before, and which left enough over to provide them with cabs when they got to London. She herself saw them into a first-class carriage marked "For Ladies only," and she gave them also into the charge of the guard, paying him five shillings in advance for looking after them. It is true she paid him this money out of the girls' own little fund, but it quite looked as if she were spending her own worldly goods for their advantage. The last thing they saw as they left the little station was her kind and yet anxious face gazing after them. She was blowing kisses to them, and wondering most anxiously what would happen between now and the evening when she was to meet their train again.

"I do feel," said Florence, as the train brought them beyond the narrow confines of the little town of Langdale, "that we are deceiving dear Mrs Fortescue most horribly."

"Well, it's no fault of ours," said Brenda; "we'll have to undeceive her to-morrow. But, after all, she won't suffer, for Mr Timmins will pay her in full for keeping us until the end of the holidays; and then, instead of going back to school, we'll begin our life's work. I do feel excited about what is going to happen to-day, don't you, Florence?"

Florence said she did, and sat book in her seat. But her thoughts were considerably absorbed with Lieutenant Reid. She was wondering what he was doing, and how he was spending his time, and considering how she would pass her own time until that day next week, when she could tell him that he might have his very heart's desire, and that a girl, poor as the poorest church mouse, would be willing to marry him.

"How glad he will be," thought Florence. "He is very nice, very nice indeed; but, of course, we must be engaged for some time before we think of marrying, for I could not leave darling Brenda until she was safely secure with some sort of livelihood."

They arrived in London between eleven and twelve o'clock, and were met at the station by one of Mr Timmins' clerks—a grave, elderly-looking man of the name of Andrews. The girls had never seen him before, but he had been given explicit directions by Mr Timmins to look out for young ladies bearing a certain appearance, and as no other girl quite so pretty as Florence stepped out of the train, he went up to her at once and asked if she was Miss Heathcote.

Florence replied in the affirmative.

They were then ushered by Mr Andrews into a very comfortable private brougham which belonged to Mr Timmins, and were taken straight to his office in Chancery Lane.

Mr Timmins was the head of a large firm of solicitors, and the girls passed through many rooms full of clerks, both old and young, who looked up as they passed by and gazed at them with admiration. Even Brenda was a pretty girl, but Florence was quite above the ordinary with regard to good looks. There was something so fresh and innocent, and withal pathetic, about the young creatures, that the men who watched them felt their hearts softening both with admiration and affection. Those who were old thought that they would like such girls to be their daughters, and those who were young felt instinctively that such girls would make good wives and sisters. The girls passed through the different rooms, and were presently ushered into Mr Timmins' own private sanctum.

He was waiting for them, and was quite alone. He gave them both a very hearty welcome, and desired them to take off their hats and jackets and sit near the fire. Brenda obeyed at once, but Florence looked restless and impatient.

"I suppose," she said, after a minute's pause, while she was fiddling with a feather boa which she wore round her neck, "you will tell us to-day, Mr Timmins, just what we are to do in the future."

"I have sent for you for that purpose," he replied.

"We have got to earn our living, haven't we?" said Florence.

"Well," he replied, speaking slowly, "girls who have no money have, as a rule, to earn their living."

Florence looked at Brenda and half smiled, but Brenda's sweet face was very grave.

"Sit down, Florence," she said: "don't be impatient. Let us wait until we hear what Mr Timmins has to say."

"Yes; that is quite right, Brenda," said Mr Timmins. "Florence, please take your sealskin jacket off, and your hat: you will be much too hot in this room if you don't." Florence now hesitated no longer. She took her pretty cap off, pushed back her chestnut hair, and unfastened her sealskin jacket. She then sank book in the easy-chair provided for her by Mr Timmins.

"Now, my dears," said the good man, "I told you the other day that I would send for you when I had something in my mind's eye for your benefit; and I think I have something. It is my proposal, therefore, that we shall first of all partake of a little lunch. You must be very hungry, both of you, for I know you started from Langdale at nine o'clock; and afterwards we will go to see Lady Marian Dixie."

"But what can she want with us?" said Brenda.

"She will tell you herself," said Mr Timmins, in his grave voice.

"And we have just seventy-five pounds to live on," said Florence. "It seems a good deal of money, for although, Mr Timmins, although you were always very generous, you did not give us a lot of pocket money; you just bought our clothes for us, and paid our school bills, and paid Mrs Fortescue in the holidays; but we ourselves never had much, had we, Brenda?"

"Good gracious!" said Mr Timmins—he threw up his hands as he spoke—"you cost hundreds a year, girls—hundreds a year."

"Then," said Florence, still speaking gravely and taking the lead, which completely astonished her sister Brenda, "don't you think you did exceedingly wrong to waste all that money on us when you knew that by and by we should have nothing?"

Mr Timmins turned rather red.

"I sent you the account in full, didn't I, Brenda?" he said.

"You sent me an account," said Brenda; "but, to tell you the truth, I haven't read it yet."

"Oh!" said Mr Timmins, with a groan. "How exactly like all other women you are. Nothing will make a woman careful with regard to money. The fact is, she needs a husband to look after her. I wish you two were provided with good husbands, that I do. But there—no one will look at a penniless girl in these days, even though she is as pretty as my friend Florence."

Florence coloured very high. She looked full at Brenda. Then she said quickly—

"There is one man who will look at a penniless girl, and marry her too, if she wishes to marry him."

"What do you mean?" said Mr Timmins. "I am glad you have spoken of it, Florence," said Brenda. "Even if you had not, I should feel it my duty to do so."

"Oh, tell him yourself, tell him yourself!" said Florence. She sprang from her seat by the fire. "Tell Him when I am not in the room. I want him to know: I want you two to talk it over. Is there no private room where I can go while you are talking it over, Mr Timmins? Is this your only private room?" Mr Timmins looked quite excited: nay, more—he looked delighted.

"Do you see that door, Florence?" he said. "Open it; and you will find a little room with a fire. A clerk may be sitting at his table writing letters for me, but he won't trouble you. Here is to-day's copy of *The Times*, my dear: you can take this with you to read. An intelligent, well-educated girl ought to read her *Times* every day. I have ordered lunch to be here in a quarter of an hour; so you had better go at once if you really wish Brenda to tell me your story."

Florence got up. She felt red all over. There was a tingling sensation down her back. She was half ashamed and half proud. Her lover was assuming a magnitude in her eyes. He must really be a most heroic person to wish to marry her even though she had not a penny.

According to Mr Timmins, men never did marry penniless girls in these days, even though the girls were beautiful.

She quickly reached the shelter of the little room, shut the door behind her and, sitting down with her back to the clerk, pretended to read *The Times*. Meanwhile, Mr Timmins turned anxiously to Brenda.

"What does this mean? what is it, Brenda?" he said. "Why, Flo—she is quite a child: how old is she, Brenda?"

"Eighteen," said Brenda at once. "Just a year younger than I am."

"Well, tell me all about it."

"I will tell you what I know," said Brenda. "We have been, as you know, visitors at Langdale for several years. It is true that Mrs Fortescue has taken us to the seaside in the summer, but we have invariably spent our Easter and Christmas holidays at Langdale, and we have got to know the people. In especial, we have got to know the Arbuthnots, who are, in my opinion, absolutely sweet; and there are the Misses Salter, who are very kind and very, very nice; and there is Major Reid—a dear old gentleman—and Major Reid's son. It is about Major Reid's son I want to tell you."

"Yes—yes!" said Mr Timmins, in an impatient and very anxious voice.

"He is in the Army," continued Brenda. "He is quite young—I don't know his age, but he cannot be twenty-five yet. He is a lieutenant in one of His Majesty's regiments of foot, and we have known him since he was a young lad and we were children. I never did notice that he especially cared about Florence; but this Christmas his manners were completely changed—in fact, the other day, he asked her to marry him."

"Thinking that she would be an heiress, no doubt, the young scoundrel!" said Mr Timmins, with an angry twist of his person as he spoke.

"Oh no; there you wrong him. He told Florence most emphatically that he cared for her only for herself, and he would marry her gladly if she were as poor as a church mouse. Now, I don't know why church mice should be especially poor; but that was his expression, and it has had a great weight with Florence, who knew the truth all the time, but could not tell him on account of her promise to you."

"Ha!" said Mr Timmins. "She never told him—the little witch—did she?"

"Of course she didn't. She had faithfully promised you not to breathe it to a soul."

"And what sort is he, Brenda? You can tell me, because you are not in love with him. Now, give me a fair and unbiassed opinion of what sort the young man is."

"He is quite good-looking, and quite gentlemanly," said Brenda at once. "His father is a dear old gentleman, and I believe the family is a good one. He is the only child, and his mother has been dead for a long time. His father thinks a lot about Michael, I know."

"Then I suppose the father will be able to leave the son something?"

"I don't know anything about that. I fancy they are both poor. Major Reid has his pension, of course, but I should not imagine they have much private means. They live in a little house, but they are quite nice people."

"You wouldn't mind your sister marrying him, would you?"

"Not if she loved him."

"Thank you very much, Brenda. You can't tell me any more for the present."

"Do you think he will propose to her when he knows—or rather do you think he will renew his proposal?" asked Brenda anxiously.

"That remains to be proved, my dear. Ah! here comes lunch. We will, for the time at least, consider that the young man is faithful and means what he says. Time alone can prove what his true sentiments are. Call your sister back; this will make a little change in my arrangements for you both."

Florence re-entered the room. She had not found the copy of the day's *Times* particularly interesting. Her cheeks were still flushed. She looked with apprehension at Mr Timmins, but kind Mr Timmins patted her on the shoulder and said, "Good girl, good girl!" in an appreciative way, which put her at her ease at once; so much so, that she thoroughly enjoyed the very excellent repast which was sent in from a neighbouring restaurant, and of which both girls ate with appetite. When it was over, Mr Timmins said—

"Now, my dears, I want to say something to you."

They both looked at him attentively.

"I am going to take you, Florence, and you, Brenda, to see my old friend, Lady Marian Dixie. She is an elderly woman and full of the milk of human kindness. She will talk to you herself, and I will not tell you beforehand what she is likely to say: indeed, it would be difficult for me to do so, for I do not know myself. Afterwards, the probabilities are that you, Florence, will go back to Langdale, and that Brenda will stay with Lady Marian."

"What?" said Brenda with a start.

Mr Timmins looked at her with affection.

"That is what is most likely to happen," he said: "but I can't tell you anything. You must both be obedient and good, for the present, and allow me to guide you. I have your very best interests at heart. I am a friend to you both, as I was to your father and your mother before you. Lady Marian also knew your mother well. Don't forget that when you are talking to her to-day."

"And I," said Florence, "am I to tell Mrs Fortescue—"

"Nothing of the sort, my dear: I should be sorry to give you such a piece of work. I will myself write to Mrs Fortescue, and tell her that her services, as far as you both are concerned, will come to an end on the twentieth of January, that Brenda has found a home—as I expect will be probable—with Lady Marian Dixie, and that she will be paid for you both until that date."

"And I?" said Florence, once more.

"Ah, Florence," said the old lawyer; "better things may be in store for you; but time will prove. There is nothing, my dear, in all the world, like disinterested affection, like the true, true homage of the heart, which has nothing to do with money nor outward accessories. In fact, my dear girls, I may as well tell you that I have the greatest horror of those men who are known as fortune seekers, the men who court girls simply because they want their money. A girl who has not money has a very poor chance in the society in which she usually moves. I do not know which is the worst off, the handsome poor girl who is attracted by the rich *parvenu* and marries him for his wealth, or the handsome poor man who marries the rich girl because of her money. You, my dears, will at least be saved from this calamity. But now, come; I have ordered the brougham to be ready for us at a quarter-past one, and I think the time is up. I will ring for Andrews. You, Florence, will be on your way back to Langdale soon after three o'clock, so we have not too much time to spare."

Andrews answered the summons of his chief, and assured him that the brougham was waiting just outside the little court where the celebrated firm of Timmins and Co conducted their highly successful business. He himself accompanied his chief and the two young ladies to the carriage. Mr Timmins looked critically at his young charges.

"Is there anything you both happen to want in the world of dress?" he said. "I don't say for a single moment that you have any means to buy yourselves luxuries, but just now it might be just possible for me— Oh, by no means as a present! but, nevertheless, it might be possible for me to give you some little things that you might require. Just say the word, my dears: do not hesitate. I know girls want so many pretty things—gloves, shoes, boots, hats, handkerchiefs, etc, etc."

But the Heathcote girls assured good Mr Timmins that they were well supplied with all these necessaries. They took care to assure him that there was not a single thing that they required, and he was forced to accept their word, although he seemed more uneasy than pleased when they rejected any sort of help on his part.

They drove across St. James' Park, and then down a quiet street, until at last the carriage stopped before Lady Marian Dixie's door. Here a grave man in livery and with powdered hair immediately answered the bell. He assured Andrews that his mistress was within. Mr Timmins got out of the carriage and had a private word with him. He then turned to the girls.

"Hudson," he said, "will show you into the dining-room for a few minutes while I talk to Lady Marian."

He went upstairs quite lightly, two steps at a time, and the girls stood and faced each other in the great dining-room of the house in Cadogan Place. Florence looked full at Brenda.

"Brenda," she said, "if I had thought for a single moment that this sort of half engagement—for it scarcely amounts to that—which now exists between Michael Reid and myself would part me from you, I should never have consented to it. I don't want to go back to Langdale alone. I don't want to, I don't wish to, I won't go back without you. You must come back with me, Brenda, darling Brenda!"

"No," said Brenda; "we must do what is right: we are not choosers any longer and you know, Florence, that we are in the position of girls who have to earn their own living, and if I can earn mine here, why, I must; and if you can bring yourself to get engaged to Michael Reid, why then, some employment will be found for you until he is well enough off to marry. I assure you, Mr Timmins seemed quite pleased when he heard of all that Michael had said to you."

"I do like him myself!—the more I think of him, the more I like him," said Florence.

"But all the same," she added, "it is odious going back to Langdale without you! and then when Mrs Fortescue finds out, it will be awful, awful!"

"No: I don't think it will," said Brenda. "I am sure Mr Timmins will be exceedingly careful not to make anything awful for you, Florence. Ah! and here he comes."

The door was opened, and Mr Timmins came in. He was accompanied by a beautiful old lady, whose hair was snowy white. She wore a white cap made of Brussels lace. She was dressed in soft grey and wore a white embroidered scarf round her shoulders. Any one more elegant and altogether lovely than this old person the girls had never seen. She was as far removed from the people at Langdale as light is from darkness. Each movement was aristocratic, and in addition to that, she had one of the kindest faces in the world.

"How do you do, my dears?" she said, coming forward at once and taking a hand of each. "Now, let me guess to whom I am speaking. Yes, this must be Brenda. Brenda, you have such a look of your mother. I used to know her very, very well indeed a long time ago; and this, of course, is Florence; she has got her father's eyes. Well, come upstairs with me, dears, won't you? and let us have a chat together."

The girls followed the old lady upstairs, but when they reached the drawing-room landing, they were astonished to find that Mr Timmins had not followed them.

"Where is Mr Timmins?" asked Florence at once.

"He will see you back to the railway station presently, Florence," was Lady Marian's reply. "He would rather we had a chat all alone for the time being."

She took them both into a snug room, made them seat themselves, and then began to talk in an easy and pleasant way. When the girls had both got over their first shyness, she asked Brenda if she would come to her on a visit for three months.

"It is quite a short time," she said; "but I name three months because I know you would like a limit to the time you propose to spend with me. During that period, I hope you will consider yourself in every respect my guest. I don't offer you any salary, my dear, but I will give you what clothes are necessary, and you in return will write some letters for me and occasionally read aloud to me. I hope to make you quite happy. I would do more, far more than this for your mother's daughter."

"But what about Florence?" said Brenda, her pretty eyes filling with tears.

"Ah well," said Lady Marian; "I did intend to offer the same hospitality to Florence, and she is at liberty to come to me if she wishes; but I think it is only fair to her to let her return to Langdale; at least for the present. If you do want to come to me, Florence, you have only to send me a letter."

"To come on a visit?" asked Florence.

"Well, yes," said the old lady. "I do not want a companion. You see, I have my maid Pearson, who has been with me for many long years, and who understands all my requirements. But I will do far you what I do for your sister, and it is only a matter of three months. At the end of that time you must, of course, both of you find some means of earning your living."

Florence rose proudly to her feet.

"Very well," she said. "I do not think I will trouble you."

There was a distressed look on her face, and Brenda never felt nearer crying in the whole course of her life.

"Oh, Florence," she said, "I would give all the wide world to be going back with you to Langdale to-day!" Then she turned to Lady Marian. "I know well," she said, "that you mean to be kind, but you cannot possibly tell what this means to homeless girls who have never been parted before in the whole course of their lives."

"I can quite understand what you are suffering, dear," said Lady Marian; "but we all have to go through pain; it is part of our great purgatory, but it draws out the good in us and develops qualities which without it might perish. Now I know you have plenty to say to each other, and Mr Timmins will come back for Florence in less than an hour. I will leave you here to talk to each other until he arrives."

As Lady Marian spoke, she left the room. The moment they were alone, Florence flung herself into Brenda's arms and burst out crying.

"I never felt so wretched in all my life!" she said. "I almost hate Michael! But for him I should be staying with you here; and yet how could I stay just on a visit with that old lady? It is all very well for her to say that she was a friend of our mother's, but she is no friend of ours."

"She seems very kind, very kind indeed," said Brenda; "and I know she will be good to me. I will write to you every day, Florence."

"Yes, do," said Florence. "But oh! I am a miserable girl!"

She cried long and hard, and when at last Mr Timmins came to fetch her, her face was quite disfigured by her bitter sobbing.

"Come, come," he said, "this will never do. You will smile at this dark hour some day, Miss Florence. But now we have just barely time to reach the railway station. I am going to send Andrews with you as far as Langdale, as I prefer your not travelling alone." Florence could not help thinking how strange the circumstances of their lives had become. They were very poor girls. They were absolutely without a penny in the world—that is, almost without a penny; and yet they had to travel first-class, and one girl would not be allowed to go back to Langdale alone. She turned to Mr Timmins. An idea came to her.

"If we are to be poor," she said, "and to earn our living, why don't you let us begin at once? It is far, far kinder than allowing us to spend our last penny and then starting us on this cold world with nothing to protect us against its rebuffs."

"But you, Florence," said the old man, "have secured the love of an honest heart. You surely, at least, are not to be pitied."

"That is true," she said; and the thought certainly did give her comfort. Michael—dear, handsome Michael—wished her to be as poor as a church mouse. Well, she was: there was no doubt of that.

As Mr Timmins was parting from her at the railway station, he slipped ten pounds into her hand.

"You must have a little ready money to spend," he said. "Be exceedingly careful of it."

"Is it part of our seventy-five pounds?" she asked.

He nodded. There was a strange expression on his face.

"Good-bye for the present, dear child," he said. "Tell Mrs Fortescue to-night when you see her, that your sister is staying with Lady Marian Dixie, and that I will write to her myself to-morrow or next day. It is quite unnecessary that she should know anything about your circumstances. Whatever you do in the future, Langdale is scarcely likely to be your home."

Chapter Seven.

An Exchange of Confidences.

While the girls were in London, Mrs Fortescue had by no means passed an idle day. She had meant to visit several friends with the avowed intention of talking about her young heiresses, as she invariably alluded to Brenda and Florence. She would at least amuse herself hinting at the possibilities which lay before her; but it so happened that she had scarcely got through her ordinary household duties before she had an unexpected visitor. This was no less a person than Major Reid.

Major Reid was, as a rule, considered a woman-hater. Since the death of his wife he had certainly never paid attentions to any woman. On the contrary, he had avoided the society of the fair sex, and had employed himself in his library and garden, living almost entirely alone, except when his son bore him company. For him to visit Mrs Fortescue, therefore, on this special day was a great surprise to the good lady.

She had not the least idea that Michael Reid cared for Florence. She had, it is true, observed his attentions to her on Christmas Eve, but had not given them any serious thought. The young man was an acknowledged flirt, and was fond of the society of all pretty girls; and what pretty girl at Langdale could compare with Florence? That she had taken a walk with him on the following day had scarcely aroused any suspicions. The young people were old friends. Florence would make a great match some day. So beautiful, so rich, so well-born— what had she not to give a husband? Poor Michael Reid would indeed be a silly man if he fell in love with a girl like Florence. The visit, therefore, of Major Reid did not in the least connect itself with Florence in Mrs Fortescue's mind.

She was up in her bedroom rearranging some of her drawers; for she was a very busy, active little woman, who kept her place in immaculate order and never was a moment unemployed. She was so engaged when Bridget came to inform her that Major Reid would like to see her in the drawing-room.

"Dear, dear!" thought Mrs Fortescue. "What does the man want?"

She said aloud to Bridget—

"Go down to the Major; give him my compliments, and say that I will be with him in a moment."

She then proceeded to put on a clean collar and a fresh and becoming tie of cherry-coloured ribbon at her throat. Her dress was dark brown. She looked a very neat and comely little person when she entered the Major's presence. The Major, however, had no special eye for Mrs Fortescue's comeliness. He looked rather excited. He was holding his stick in his hand as though he did not wish to part with it, and when he stood up, it was with considerable difficulty that Mrs Fortescue could get him to sit down again.

"Dear, dear!" he said. "Dear, dear! I don't know how to apologise for coming to you at such an hour before lunch. I do hope you will forgive me."

Here he deliberately paced from the door to the mantelpiece. The room was small, and he accomplished the distance in a couple of strides; but his whole manner was so confused and *distrait* that Mrs Fortescue wondered if the good man had taken leave of his senses and was about to propose to her. She was, however, thoroughly sensible and practical; and, knowing that the Major had certainly no money wherewith to support a second wife, turned her mind from the subject and endeavoured to set him at his ease.

"Do sit down," she said. "Do you know—I am sorry to have to say it—but it fidgets me dreadfully to see people pacing about my drawing-room."

The Major dropped in the nearest chair as though he had been shot.

"May I take your stick from you?" said Mrs Fortescue.

He resigned it with the expression of one who was about to suffer martyrdom.

"Now, that is much better," she said. "But I would suggest an easy-chair; there is one near the window. You can then lean back and cross your legs. My late dear husband said he never felt comfortable unless he could lean back in his chair and cross his legs. Ah! how well I remember him; such a dear fellow, so devoted to me. I have never ceased to mourn for him. I could never put another in his place."

"Now I have set him at his ease, and got him to abandon the ridiculous idea of proposing to me," thought the widow. "Yes; he looks quite happy, but I do wonder what he wants. I could have taken the opportunity in the absence of the dear girls of looking over the house linen; but he will dawdle on—I know he will. What can he have to say?"

The Major was staring hard at Mrs Fortescue, but she soon perceived that though he was looking at her, he was not seeing her. He was, in fact, looking through her at something which considerably disturbed, excited, and delighted him.

"The Heathcotes have gone to London, have they not?" he said.

"Yes," she replied at once. "My children have left me for the day; but they are coming back to-night—my Brenda and my Florence, as I call them—for they are to me, I assure you, Major Reid, just as though they were my very own children. For years I have given them a mother's care, and—sweet girls!—they have repaid me amply."

"They are fine girls, both of them," said the Major.

"Fine!" said Mrs Fortescue. "I should scarcely express what the girls are by that word. Aristocratic—I should call them; more particularly Florence, and yet in some ways Brenda has a rare dignity of her own —like a sweet winter rose: that is what I call her; whereas Florence is like the passion-flower. Marvellous grace that child possesses! He certainly will be a happy man who secures her."

"I am coming to that," said Major Reid. "I am coming to that. I want to confide in you."

Mrs Fortescue became intensely interested. She had not looked for a confidence in this visit of the Major's; but now she saw by his red face and by the way his lips twitched that he had really come on special business.

"The fact is this," he said. "That young dog of mine, Michael, has had the audacity to fall in love with your—well, your adopted child. He is madly in love with Florence, and I have an idea that she responds to his attachment. There; I have told you the truth. I thought it only right."

"You will excuse me for a minute," said Mrs Fortescue.

She got up abruptly and left the room. The moment she had done so, the Major sprang from his easy-chair, took hold of his stick, and began to pace about more energetically than ever.

"If that woman puts a spoke in Mike's wheel, I shall hate her as long as I live!" he thought. "She is just the spiteful sort to do it. I shall have to be very wary when I talk to her."

Meanwhile, Mrs Fortescue had really left the room to recover her self-control. But she was a woman, and could quickly achieve her object.

She came back looking as calm as though the Major had not brought her any special information.

"You will, Major Reid, forgive me," she said, "for having left you so suddenly, but your news startled me."

"Naturally, quite naturally," he answered.

He was clasping his stick between his two hands and leaning on it. His stick gave him a lot of support.

"Quite naturally," he repeated.

"As my dear Florence's mother—we will assume for the time being that I hold that position—you are quite right to tell me, Major Reid. But when—when did Michael give my dear girl to understand that he cared for her!"

"As far as I can make out, he has always cared for her," said the Major; "but I don't think he showed her any serious attention until Christmas Day. You must have noticed that they were a good deal together then."

"Oh well—I naturally observed that your son was pleased to be with the prettiest girl in the room."

"Quite so; most natural, most natural," said the Major. "Well, yesterday they took a walk together, and then he told her that he—he loved her."

"He ought to have spoken to me or to Mr Timmins."

"I don't agree with you, madam," said the Major. "I think the person most concerned ought to be first talked to on so essential a matter. My boy is the very soul of honour. You know what a good family we belong to. The Reids of Ardnacarrick can hold up their heads with any one. It is true, I am only the younger son; but there is never any saying what my boy may inherit by and by. Anyhow, he is a good boy, a brave boy, a true soul. He spoke openly to the girl, and she—"

"Yes; that is the important part," said Mrs Fortescue. "What did Florence say?"

"She was wonderfully careful, all things considered."

"I have taught her that," said Mrs Fortescue, drawing herself up. "I have taught her that of all qualities self-control is the most essential in the case of a woman."

"She asked him," continued the Major, "to give her a week to decide. She has gone to town to-day. Most probably she will tell her guardian."

"Oh dear, oh dear!" said Mrs Fortescue. Then she added, the colour rushing into her cheeks: "Do you think it was quite fair of your son to try to entangle Florence before she met any other man?"

"Madam," said Major Reid, "I must not permit such a word. You must excuse me if I ask you to recall it. The Reids of Ardnacarrick may very justly unite themselves with any family in England."

"I am saying nothing against you, Major; nor indeed against your son. But Florence has only just left school: she is but eighteen years of age, and will be, I understand, exceedingly well off. She has also great beauty. My hope was that I could take a house in London during the spring and bring both girls out."

"Yes!" said the Major, his face hot with indignation. "And marry Florence to some dissipated *roué* or some horrible American millionaire! My son is a gentleman, and surely," he added, the anxiety in his face causing him to clutch his stick more violently than ever, "they will have money enough between them."

"I do not know," said Mrs Fortescue, "why you call it between them, when it happens to be entirely on one side."

The Major was quite silent for a minute. He felt the indignity of his present position, and would have given a good deal to put himself outside Mrs Fortescue's house at the present moment. But as he had come there with the express intention of finding out what Florence's fortune would be, it seemed absurd to go away without doing so. Accordingly, he said, after a pause—

"My dear madam, we have known each other for years."

"We have," said Mrs Fortescue.

"And neither you nor I are to blame if the young people fall in love with each other."

"That is certainly true," said Mrs Fortescue. "I never encouraged it."

"Oh!" said the Major. "Can you say that? You were always asking my boy over to play tennis or croquet with the girls during their holidays: in fact, he was always in and out of the house. He was the only young man you admitted into their society."

"True—very true," she said. "I did wrong; I did not think. I hope, Major, you won't use this knowledge to my disadvantage."

"By no means," he replied. "I should be more than sorry to injure your position at the present moment: my entire desire, my one object is to be as friendly with you as possible. I have come to you at the first possible moment to tell you what I myself know—that the young people are much attracted each to the other, and that a marriage is likely to take place between them. It is impossible for either you or me to prevent such a union: indeed, we should be doing wrong were we to attempt it. It is best, therefore, for us to be friends in the matter. Two heads are better than one. Florence need never be ashamed of herself as Mrs Reid. As my daughter-in-law she will have a good position, and as my son's wife she will be a truly happy woman. You can, of course, make yourself disagreeable at the present moment, but that will not prevent the marriage; for, after all, you were only paid to be good to the girls."

Mrs Fortescue sprang indignantly to her feet. People never spoke directly about money at Langdale. No one ever before had alluded to the fact that she had made a nice harvest out of the girls. No one had been so ill-bred; but now it flashed across her mind that it was true: it also came over her that she had been envied amongst the most aristocratic members of society in Langdale, because of her chaperonage of Brenda and Florence Heathcote. Accordingly, she sank down again with a faint smile on her face.

"After all," she said, her words coming out with a pause between each, "we had best, as you say, be friendly in the matter."

"Yes; that is just what I think. I can help you if you can help me—"

"Won't you stay and have lunch with me?" said Mrs Fortescue suddenly.

The Major loathed having lunch anywhere except at home, where he invariably ate a chop specially prepared, and drank a glass of old port. The present occasion was too serious, however, to make him consider either his chop or port.

"I shall be delighted to have lunch with you," he said.

Mrs Fortescue thought of her cold mutton and the very sour claret which she usually had on the sideboard but never drank. Still, what did food matter? The moment was too important. She reflected with satisfaction that she had one or two bottles of champagne in her wine cellar. She would have one opened for the Major. He was fond of good champagne—that she knew. Afterwards he would talk to her; they would, as he expressed it, get to understand each other.

She left the room to give some directions with regard to lunch, and came back in a few minutes ready to listen to the Major. On purpose, she drew him into other channels of conversation, chatting lightly and agreeably about the girls and about other matters, even going to the length of asking his advice as to what port of town would be the best for her to take a house for the coming season.

Lunch, after all, was a poor affair, when it did arrive; but the Major gallantly ate his cold mutton and drank enough champagne to put him into good humour.

After the meal was over, they went into the drawing-room again, where excellent black coffee was served, and then the Major found courage to ask Mrs Fortescue that question which was burning on the top of his tongue.

"You know," he said, "that my boy Michael could not possibly marry at present, deeply as he loves Florence, were she not an heiress."

"I quite understand that," said Mrs Fortescue.

"You, my dear madam, probably know something of what her expectations are. She is a very young girl, only eighteen, but there is no sense in her waiting to marry until she is twenty-one; for marriage, as a rule, has an equal effect with coming of age, as far as money is concerned. Can you give me the least idea what she is likely to inherit?"

"No; I can't," said Mrs Fortescue bluntly. "I have often and often tried to find out, but have never succeeded. My idea, however, is—seeing that the girls have been spared no expense whatever since the death of their parents, and knowing that their parents, during their lifetime, were very well off—that they will both be rich. I know that Mr Timmins has spent hundreds a year on their education, and as to the amount he has devoted to their dress, it has really amazed me, although it has been no affair of mine. Florence now possesses a set of sealskin which would delight any duchess in the land, and there was a little talk last year of giving her a similar set of chinchilla. She looks better in furs than her sister, who requires altogether a simpler style of dress. The girls travelled up to town first-class to-day and were met by Mr Timmins' man—his confidential clerk: that I happen to know; but I have not the slightest idea whether Florence Heathcote's fortune represents a pound a year, or two or three thousand."

"Two or three thousand!" murmured the Major.

A greedy look came into his old eyes. He suddenly rose to his feet.

"I am very much obliged," he said. "You have frankly told me all you know."

"Most frankly; most unreservedly. You will regard our conversation as confidential?"

"Certainly: it would not be fair to mention it to anybody else until the week for which Florence has stipulated expires," said the old man. "But now; let me assure you, that were the dear girl blessed with nothing at all in the way of money she would be equally precious both to my son and to me."

"Oh, you old hypocrite!" murmured Mrs Fortescue under her breath, but she did not say the words aloud: people don't in polite society.

The Major took his leave.

"Your champagne was excellent," he said, as the widow saw him to the door. "You must let me know some day where you get it, and, of course, when the week is up and everything is comfortably arranged, you and Brenda and Florence will give us the pleasure of dining with us at the Moat."

"Thank you so much, Major," said Mrs Fortescue.

The Major walked down the street, murmuring to himself—

"Two or three thousand a year! It is true—it must be true. She has practically admitted it."

He met his son, who was, in fact, waiting for him.

"Come for a walk, Mike," said the old man. "Give me your arm, my boy. I have been busy over your affairs during the morning, and the fact is, that woman's sweet champagne has got into my head. I can't imagine how it is that women never know the difference between dry champagne and sweet. I shall have a bilious attack after this, as sure as fate."

"Where in the world have you been, dad?" said the lieutenant, looking with apprehension at his father's flushed face.

"Why, my boy," said the Major, "I have been eating the most abominable lunch I ever tasted in the whole course of my life at Mrs Fortescue's."

"At Mrs Fortescue's?" said the young man. "You surely have not been there about—about Florence and me!"

"Yes, I have, Mike, and you can't blame me; and I have got the most satisfactory information for you. The girl's income will run into thousands, my boy—yes, into thousands." Now, of course, Lieutenant Reid was delighted to hear this, but he felt all the same annoyed at his father's lack of circumspection in going to see Mrs Fortescue.

"The news will be all over the place," he said. "That woman is the most inveterate gossip in Langdale. She will tell all her friends just what has happened, and if Flo chooses to give me up, you will be the one to blame."

"Oh, she won't give you up. She loves you dearly, my boy; and no other, no other," said the Major. "I really congratulate you, Mike; and if there is any possible way in which I can help you at the present moment, you have but to command it. Some thousands a year! Three, four, five—I should not be the least surprised if it was five thousand a year. The girls have been brought up as if they might expect that income at the very least. You're a lucky dog—a very lucky dog, Mike."

Chapter Eight.

A Tempting Tea.

Mrs Fortescue's morning had been so exciting that she really could not settle down at searching through her house linen for possible or impossible holes during the afternoon. It was her bounden duty to go to see the Arbuthnots. She ought to visit them after the delightful dinner they had given her on Christmas Day. Accordingly, putting on her most becoming dress, she started off between three and four o'clock in the direction of their house. She must meet the train which would bring her darlings back to her between six and seven, but during the intervening hours she might spend her time quite comfortably with Susie, chatting to her, of course—not on *the* subject, but on every possible subject which led towards it, approaching it, as it were, by every devious path within her knowledge.

Susie was upright, honest as the day. Mrs Fortescue was a crooked-minded woman; but very straight people are, as a rule, apt not to see the crookedness of their friends. Susie liked every one at Langdale, just as much as the Colonel liked them. She was heartily pleased to see her friend, and told her so, frankly. Susie was not wearing her grey barège, and the supporting silk lining could not therefore sustain her; but she was very neatly dressed in an old black serge which she had altered with her own clever fingers, and which fitted her plump form to perfection. Round her neck she were a neat linen collar, and had linen cuffs round her plump wrists. Her hands were ringless and very fat. Her face, always highly coloured, was a little redder than usual, because she had been taking advantage of the fine morning and spending it in the garden. She loved gardening, and there was not a day, either summed or winter, which did not give her something to do in her favourite employment.

"Now," she said, when she saw Mrs Fortescue; "this *is* good! You have come to tea, of course. I will order some hot cakes. They can be made in a twinkling. I have desired cook to do them from a new recipe which I happened to cut out of a penny paper last week. How nice you look, Mrs Fortescue! and how are the darling girls? What a decided beauty Florence is turning into!"

"Of course you know," said Mrs Fortescue, throwing meaning into her tone, "that both girls went to London this morning to spend the day with their guardian and lawyer, Mr Timmins, of Pye's Court."

"No, I didn't know it," said Susie. Then she added, seeing that something was expected of her: "Did they go alone?"

"Well, they went together first-class, and were met at the station by Mr Timmins' confidential clerk. They are coming back to night."

"Dear children!" said Susie, in her sweet voice. "I am so fond of them both."

"And they are fond of you, Susie."

"I wonder what they will do in the future," said Susie. "Is it really true that they have left school?"

"Yes, it is quite true," said Mrs Fortescue. "I am sorry," answered Susie.

"Sorry? What do you mean? Florence is eighteen and Brenda nineteen."

"Yes," said Susie; "but one only begins to appreciate school at that age. Before, one is too young and lessons seem a useless drudgery. One's mind is not big enough or broad enough to take in the advantages of learning. It is a great, great pity that Mr Timmins does not give them two more years at Newnham or Girton or some such place."

"Oh, my dear?" said Mrs Fortescue, throwing up her hands. "How can you say anything so horrible! Newnham or Girton! They would be simply ruined; and men do so hate learned women."

"Do they?" said Susie. She paused reflectively. "I have known one or two," she said, after a pause, "whom men have loved very much. I don't think it is the learning part that men hate; it is something else which now and then the learned woman possesses. Perhaps it is pride in her own attainments. Surely no sensible man can dislike a woman for knowing things."

"They do—they all do," said Mrs Fortescue. "My dear late lamented did. He told me he could not even have looked at me if I had had a smattering of Latin or Greek; and I have heard many other men say the same."

"Then they must be quite worthless," said Susie, "and we needn't bother about them. Ah! and here comes the tea. Put it here, please, Peters."

The servant arranged the very tempting tea on a little table, and Susie stood up to perform her duties as hostess. She was certainly remarkably plain, but, somehow, no one ever thought her plain when they looked at her, for goodness shone out of her eyes and seemed to radiate from her stout little person. Mrs Fortescue was quite ready to do justice to the excellent tea, the rich cream, the plum cake, and that new recipe for hot cakes which Susie's cook had so successfully carried out and which resulted in such appetising, melting morsels, that the good woman was consoled for the loss of one of her few bottles of champagne, and for the fact that she knew very well that Major Reid had hated his lunch.

"Do you know," she said, as she finished her meal, "that I never enjoy my tea anywhere as I do here. Besides, I had a hot lunch to-day. Who do you think came and had lunch with me?"

"How can I guess?" said Susie. "I suppose you were all alone, as the girls were in London."

"No: I was not alone. I had a visitor—a man."

"A man?" said Susie, opening her round eyes.

"Yes; no less a person than Major Reid. Now, what do you think of that?"

"Oh; I like him very much," said Susie.

"Do you, now? I wonder why?"

"Why," said Susie, "because I think he is nice. He is very poor, of course, but he makes the best of his poverty, and he is very intelligent and fond of reading."

"Perhaps you like Michael too," said Mrs Fortescue.

"I am exceedingly fond of Michael," said Susie. "He is a dear boy."

"A boy?" said Mrs Fortescue. "Do you call him that? He is a man; he is twenty-four."

"I call twenty-four quite a boy," answered Susie. "Mike is a great friend of mine: we have always been chums, and always will be, for that matter."

Mrs Fortescue sat quite still. She longed to add something further; but Susie sat smiling to herself, for she remembered Michael's request that he might take Florence into dinner on Christmas night, and she also remembered the fact that he had walked through the snow and slush in order to secure his heart's desire. It would in Susie's eyes be a delightful match if Mike and Florence married. But she was not going

77

to speak of it. Mrs Fortescue's small black eyes sparkled.

"Well, well," she said; "we all have our tastes. I will own that in a place like Langdale one is apt to appreciate any fairly good-looking young man. But out in the great world where one meets them in shoals—simply in shoals—a person like Michael Reid would not have much chance."

"Do you think so?" said Susie very quietly. "I am sorry for the great world, then."

"You know nothing about it, Susie."

"That is true," answered Susie, who might have retorted, "No more do you," but it was not her habit ever to say anything unkind.

"Well," said Mrs Fortescue, "I suppose I must be going. I have to meet the dear girls, and they will have lots to tell me. In all probability, Susie, I shall be leaving Langdale myself this spring, for no doubt Mr Timmins will wish me to undertake the chaperonage of my two sweet girls until they marry. I look to their both making great matches, with their wealth and good looks; for they are both good-looking. They ought to do exceedingly well in the marriage market."

"If you mean by that," said Susie, the colour rushing into her face, "that they will marry men worthy of them—I mean good in the best sense of the word—good, and true and brave, then I trust they will. But if you mean anything else, Mrs Fortescue; if you mean men who will seek them for their wealth—for I presume they are rich, although really I know nothing about it, and what is more, I don't care—then I sincerely trust they won't marry that sort of man."

"Oh," said Mrs Fortescue, "you don't understand—you don't care whether they are rich or not—"

"Not one scrap," said Susie. "How can riches add to the brightness of Florence's eyes or the affection of Brenda's manner? But if riches make them a little more comfortable, I hope they will have sufficient, though we don't require much money, do we, Mrs Fortescue? I know that is not what the world would call rich," (Mrs Fortescue hated Susie for making this remark) "and most certainly father and I are not. We just contrive and contrive, and always have enough for a jolly Christmas dinner when we can really entertain our friends. I don't believe any two people in all the world are happier than my darling dad and myself, and it doesn't come from riches, for we have to be very careful. Oh, no; rich people are not the happiest, I do assure you on that point."

Mrs Fortescue could not help saying, "I do not agree with you, Susie," and she could not help giving a contemptuous glance at the old-fashioned, very plump little figure with the red face and honest round eyes. But having eaten as much as she could of Susie's very excellent food, and found it quite impossible to draw Susie Arbuthnot into any conversation of what she considered a truly interesting nature, she left the house and amused herself doing some shopping until it was time to go to the railway station to meet the girls.

There Florence alone confronted her—Florence, with a white and anxious face, although all trace of that fit of weeping which had overcome her when she parted from Brenda had disappeared from her features.

"Why, Flo—Flo, darling! Where is your sister? Where is my Brenda?"

"Brenda is staying for a few days with Lady Marian Dixie."

"But I knew nothing of this. She did not take up any clothes."

"We are to send her some. Mr Timmins has sent his clerk down with me, and he is coming back to the house with us now in order that I may pack some of Brenda's things and send them to town by him. If we are quick we shall catch the half-past seven train, and she will get what things she most requires by to-night."

"I have a cab waiting for you, my love. This is very unexpected. Did you say Lady Marian Dixie?"

"Yes," said Florence; "an old friend of my mother's."

"Well, you will have a great deal to tell me," said Mrs Fortescue; "and how very tired you look, dear."

"I am not specially tired, but I should like to get home as fast as possible in order to give Andrews a trunk full of clothes to take back to Brenda."

"Oh, surely Brenda won't be away so long as that."

Florence made no reply. She motioned to Andrews to get on the box beside the driver, and they returned to Mrs Fortescue's house almost in silence. Mrs Fortescue felt that something had happened, but did not dare to inquire. She kept repeating to herself at intervals during their drive back—

"Lady Marian Dixie—a friend of the girls' mother! It sounds very nice;

still, it is queer. Surely, surely Mr Timmins could not be so mad as to allow Lady Marian to conduct the girls about in London society! It would be too cruel to me, after all I have done for them."

When they reached the house, the cabman was desired to wait. Florence ran up to their room and, with Mrs Fortescue's help, filled a trunk with Brenda's smartest things. Mrs Fortescue talked all the time, but Florence was almost silent. The trunk was speedily packed, and the old clerk took it back to London with him.

Then the two ladies, the old and the young, went into the drawing-room and faced each other.

Chapter Nine.

Mrs Fortescue Seeks Enlightenment.

"Now, Florence," said Mrs Fortescue, "I suppose you have got something to tell me."

"I have," answered Florence. She spoke almost flippantly. "I am very, very hungry. I hope you have a nice dinner, a specially nice dinner for us both to enjoy together to-night, Mrs Fortescue."

"I have got a duck," said Mrs Fortescue; "and ducks at present are exceedingly expensive; but I never think of expense when I am providing luxuries for you and your dear sister. You deserve all the good things of life, my darlings, and I trust they will fall to your portion. Nevertheless, I think, I do think you might have confided in me."

Florence coloured and then turned pale. She wondered if anyone had, in some miraculous way, become acquainted with the fact of their own great poverty; but no, the whole thing seemed impossible. Florence herself had been careful not to breathe a word on the subject, and she was pretty sure that Brenda had not done so. What, therefore, could Mrs Fortescue mean? As to the other matter—that which related to Lieutenant Reid, it is sad to have to confess that Florence, for the time being, had forgotten the gallant lieutenant.

"I am hungry!" she said; "and I would rather talk to you after dinner than before: that is, if you don't mind."

"I don't mind at all, dearest," said Mrs Fortescue. "You would like to go upstairs and change your travelling dress. I will send Bridget in to help you."

"Thank you," said Florence.

She was about to refuse this offer, but suddenly remembered that all her dresses fastened behind, and that she could not manage this part of her toilet now that Brenda was away. She ran upstairs at once, locked her door and flung herself on her knees by her bedside. There she uttered a strangled sort of prayer to God to give her help; but she had not been more than a minute on her knees before Bridget's knock was heard. Florence went to the door and opened it.

Bridget was always respectful to the Misses Heathcote, for they were liberal with their tips and were, she considered, exceedingly nice, lively young ladies, who made the house pleasant and enabled her to stay on with Mrs Fortescue. She would long ago have left that good lady but for the fact that the Misses Heathcote came to Langdale in the holidays, and made the place bright and cheerful, and caused her mistress to provide the best food, and, in short, to give every one in the house a good time all round.

"I have come to help you, miss," said Bridget now. "You will be that lonely without dear Miss Brenda. We none of us knew she was going to stay in town when you both left this morning."

"Oh, it's all right, Biddie dear," said Florence. "Brenda had to stay: I don't want to talk too much about it, for it makes me so very sad."

"Then it ain't all right, if it makes you sad," said Bridget.

"We have all of us to bear pain in our turn, haven't we?" said Florence, looking full at the elderly servant with her bright eyes.

"I suppose so," said Bridget, who felt interested in this talk and inclined to concur. "My poor mother, who died a very lingering and painful death, always said that pain was the will of Providence. I couldn't see it, miss; but I suppose she was right."

"Yes, Bridget," said Florence; "she was quite right. Please fasten me into my white dress—this one, please. Thank you so very much."

"We have had quite an entertaining day," said Bridget. "You wouldn't believe it—but we had company to lunch."

"Company?" said Florence, in some astonishment. "What do you mean?"

"No less a person than Major Reid." Florence felt herself colouring violently.

"He came comparatively early," continued Bridget, "and had a long talk with my missis, and afterwards stayed to lunch. I can't say there was much for lunch—only the mutton bone and some fried potatoes; but my missis got up a bottle of champagne from the wine cellar, and the Major drank three or four glasses. He was very friendly indeed with my missis, and seemed a good bit excited—indeed, they both were."

Florence longed to ask more questions, but refrained, and after a time, Bridget left the room. Then the girl stood with her hands clasped together gazing straight before her into the long mirror which was fastened to the wall. She saw a very charming reflection there. The form of a girl, with the extreme grace of youth and altogether well made, stood upright before her. She saw sparkling eyes, and a wealth of hair and delicate colour on the softly rounded cheeks. She knew that she was looking at herself, and it occurred to her all of a sudden that there was no wonder at all that Michael Reid should love her just for herself and not in the very least for her gold. Was not her face her fortune? She now felt quite gay and happy. She forgot her loneliness with regard to her sister and ran downstairs humming a gay song.

Dinner was announced almost immediately, and the two ladies went into the dining-room and partook of it. Florence was really hungry and enjoyed the carefully prepared meal. Mrs Fortescue watched her as she ate. At last the dinner came to an end and they both retired to the drawing-room.

"Now," said Mrs Fortescue, the moment the door had closed behind the two, "I must ask you, Florence, to enlighten me. There is a great deal you ought to tell me. I have been kept in the dark too long. What arrangements has Mr Timmins arrived at with regard to your future?"

"He said he would write to you. I expect you will hear from him in the morning."

"But you can tell me, darling: I need not be kept on tenter-hooks until the morning."

"I would much, much rather he told you himself," said Florence, moving restlessly in her choir.

"But why, dearest? Did he ask you not to tell me?"

"He did not exactly do that; but he said he would write. From his whole tone I know he expects me to say nothing until you hear from him."

Then Florence got up. She approached Mrs Fortescue's side, and bending down, kissed the good lady on her forehead.

"You have been very, very kind to Brenda and me," she said; "and we will never forget it, never."

"I trust indeed you won't, my dear," said Mrs Fortescue. "It is my wish to continue my kindness to you both. And now, Florence, I have something to say to you on my own account. A little bird has told me a secret with regard to you. Of course, dear—with regard to Mr Timmins, he must please himself as to whether he chooses to let me know what our future plans are to be, although I maintain that if I am kept much longer in the dark, I shall think he is not treating me fairly. But as to you and your dear sister—you, at least are different. Florence, I did not think, I could not imagine that you would have a love affair—you, such a child as you are too! and keep it dark from me."

Florence found herself blushing very hotly.

"Who told you that I had a love affair?" she said.

"My dear Florence, there is not the least manner of use in your hiding the matter from me any longer. We at Langdale know each other so well that we are, in fact, like one big family. What affects one affects all. The sorrows of one try the hearts of all the others. The joys of one equally rejoice the hearts of all the others. In your happiness, my darling, the rest of us rejoice. It was Major Reid who told me; he came himself to-day to speak of his son's attachment to you. He was delighted himself; he has a great, great affection and a deep admiration for you, Florence; and I—I also think Michael an excellent young man."

"Oh—do you?" said Florence. "Do you, really?"

She had meant to go back to her seat at the opposite side of the hearth, but instead of doing this, she now dropped on her knees close to Mrs Fortescue. She had never felt so near that good lady before— so drawn to her, so part of her: in fact, the one comfort at present in her desolate position was the knowledge of Michael's love. She must, of course, not mention her own great poverty, but she could at least listen to what Mrs Fortescue had to say about him.

"I don't mind your knowing at all," she said. "I felt shy about speaking to you, but as the Major has called, it makes all the difference. And he is not angry—really? You are quite, quite sure?"

"Sure? my dear child. I am certain the Major is delighted, Florence. He loves you as a daughter. But now, take this little chair close to me and tell me all you have to say."

Florence found that she had not a great deal to say. There was something about Mrs Fortescue which seemed to shut her up. The first dawning of that young love which had awakened in her heart did not respond to the touch of the eager, selfish, worldly woman. Of course she did love—yes, she was certain now she loved Michael; but she hated talking about him. She would rather put him in the background, and when Mrs Fortescue—instead of answering her many questions with regard to the young man's youth, his early history, his dead mother, his father when he was young, and those various things about his early life which Mrs Fortescue knew and Florence did not— preferred to talk about the girl's own future, the way Michael and she would live (as Michael would probably leave the Army), and how nice it would be to settle in Langdale, Florence found a wall of separation rising up between herself and her quondam friend. She pleaded fatigue at last, and went to her room, where she spent a great part of the night in secret tears. For, notwithstanding the fact that the Major had visited Mrs Fortescue, and that Michael himself had told Florence that he would love her just the same if she were as poor as a church mouse, Florence felt certain that neither the Major nor Mrs Fortescue thought of her as a desirable wife for the young man except as a rich heiress.

"Well," she said to herself finally, as she turned on her pillow for the fifth time, "if, after hearing everything, he cares for me, I will stick to him and work hard to save a little money until we can marry; but if he doesn't—oh, oh—"

Florence would not allow herself even to finish the latter thought which came into her mind.

Chapter Ten.

"As Poor as a Church Mouse."

On the following morning, Mrs Fortescue received her promised letter from Mr Timmins. He sat down to write it almost immediately he had seen Florence off by the train, and it arrived by first post the next day. Mrs Fortescue was in the habit of having her letters brought up to her bedroom, where she used to read them, luxuriously sipping her tea and eating her thin bread and butter the while.

Florence was sound asleep in bed while Mrs Fortescue was reading the most startling information she had perhaps ever got in the course of her life. Mr Timmins' letter ran as follows—

"My dear Madam,—

"I do not know whether the contents of this letter will surprise you, but, after all, they need scarcely do so, for I have never for a single moment given you to understand that you would have anything further to do with the Misses Heathcote after the period devoted to their education was over. That time has now been reached, and the sum of money left by their late father for their education has been expended in strict accordance with his directions.

"I have been happy enough to find a suitable home for the next three months for dear Brenda Heathcote, who will stay with my friend, Lady Marian Dixie, in London. Florence is at liberty to join her sister there whenever she wishes to do so. But from what I heard yesterday I rather gather that she may have inducements to remain on at Langdale for a short time. I am the last person in the world to interfere with any young girl's predilections, provided they are in themselves innocent and suitable, and from what Brenda has mentioned to me, the man who has given his heart to Florence appears to be worthy of her. He will certainly be submitted to as severe a test as can be given to any man; but if he is worthy, he will not, I am sure, regret the noble and true wife that such a beautiful and good girl as Florence Heathcote will make him. If, on the other hand, he is unworthy of her, the sooner he shows himself in his true character, the better. As you probably know of this affair, I need not allude to it further. But what I have now to say to you is that your guardianship of my wards comes to an end on the twentieth of January. Until that date, I should be glad if you would keep Florence with you, and I will, of course, pay you in full for the maintenance of both girls, as Brenda's leaving you at an earlier date was an unforeseen coincidence over which you had no control.

"You will receive your cheque weekly as heretofore, and if you have been in any way obliged to go to additional expense for the girls, pray add it to your account.

"Thanking you for all you have done for them in the past,—

"I am, yours faithfully,—

"James Timmins."

Mrs Fortescue read this letter the first time in great bewilderment of mind. She did not in the least take it in. She had, in short, to read it from three to four times before its contents were in the least made clear to her. Even then she felt, as she expressed it, all in a muddle. She was also in a great rage, and considered herself most badly treated. The fact of the girls' being poor did not once enter into her calculations. She only thought of herself. She, who had worked and slaved for these two young girls for long and anxious years, was to have nothing whatever to do with their future. They were to be handed over to nobody knew who. Brenda had already been taken from her. She was living with a rich woman—a person of title, who was doubtless paid an extravagant sum for her support. Florence might marry Michael Reid if she pleased. Where was she, Mrs Fortescue, to come in? She was left out of everything!

The angry woman was too indignant to finish her dressing. She hastily smoothed her hair, put on a becoming dressing-gown, and, with the open letter in her hand, went straight to Florence's room. She gave a peremptory knock at the door and, when the girl said "Come in," entered without ceremony.

"Mr Timmins' letter has arrived, Florence. I must say that I consider both you and your sister have treated me shamefully—shamefully!"

Florence, who was half way through her toilet, and looked very sweet and pretty with her rich hair hanging about her neck and shoulders, and in a neat white embroidered dressing-gown, sank into a choir and looked full at Mrs Fortescue.

"I thought you would be sorry," she said; "but I don't think, after all, you are as much to be pitied as we are."

"Now what in the world do you mean by that?"

"Why, didn't he tell you?" said Florence. "You said you had heard from him."

"Yes; I have. You are to stay with me till the twentieth of January, and then I have nothing further to do with you."

"But surely, surely," said Florence; "you would not wish to have anything to do with me after then, would you?"

"What in the world do you mean?" Florence coloured.

"I see he has not told you," she said. "He ought to. It was not right of him to leave it to me. But I will tell you: I don't really mind."

"Oh—do speak out, child! You keep me so frightfully in suspense I can scarcely endure myself."

"Well," said Florence, "you would not care to keep us for nothing, would you?"

"Nothing! nothing! What does the girl mean? Why, surely you are rich? I gave Major Reid to understand yesterday that your yearly income must run into four figures. We were divided as to the amount, but I thought fifteen hundred a year each. Florence, what are you alluding to?"

Florence turned very white.

"It is awful only to be cared for because one has money," she said. "Well, there is one person who cares for me quite independently of that. And now I will tell you the truth. I have not any money—that is, I have a few pounds. Mr Timmins gave me ten pounds yesterday, and I shall have a few more pounds before all our affairs are wound up, but something quite inconsiderable. I am as poor as a church mouse, and so is Brenda. Our money was spent on our education. Now it is finished, all used up. We are penniless. Now—now—you know all about us."

Florence stood up as she spoke and extended her arms wide as though to emphasise her own words.

"We are penniless," she repeated. "Now you know."

Mrs Fortescue was absolutely silent for a minute. Then she uttered a violent ejaculation and, turning round on her heel, left the room. She slammed—absolutely slammed the door after her. Florence sat very still after she had gone.

"She would like me to leave at once," thought the girl. "But Michael—

dear Michael: he at least will be true to his word. Oh, what am I to do! I hate beyond everything in the world staying here—staying on with her when she can look at me like that. Is it my fault that I am poor! I think that I am very cruelly treated."

Tears rushed to her eyes. She stayed for a time in her room, then finished her dressing. She went downstairs to breakfast. To her surprise Mrs Fortescue was not in the room. After a moment's hesitation, she rang the bell. Bridget appeared.

"What is it, missie?" she asked.

"I want my breakfast, please," said Florence.

"My missis sent to tell you that there were no fresh eggs in the house, so that perhaps you would do with the cold ham. I don't see why fresh eggs should not be bought for you, but those were her orders, I'll make you some new coffee, nice and strong, and bring it in, in a few minutes."

Florence laughed. Her laughter was almost satirical. In a short time, Bridget came in with the coffee and a bone of ham which had been cut very bare.

"I can't make out," said Bridget, "what is the matter with my missis. I never saw anybody in such a raging temper."

"But where is she?" asked Florence.

"Oh, gone out, my dear—gone out. She has been out nearly an hour."

"Did she eat any breakfast?" asked Florence.

"That she did—the eggs that were meant for you, too; for you know she never takes eggs in the winter; she considers them too dear. But she ate your eggs this morning, and said that you might do with the ham bone."

"Thank you," said Florence.

She carved a few slices from the bone, then looked up at the old servant with a smile.

"It is such a relief," she said, "not to conceal things any longer. I will tell you, Bridget. I wonder if you are going to be just as horrid to me as Mrs Fortescue."

Bridget stood stock still staring at the girl.

"The fact is," said Florence, "Brenda and I haven't got any money.

We're not heiresses at all. We are just very poor girls who have to earn our own living. We have nothing to live on—nothing at all. I expect if all were known, you have more money at the present moment than I have, Bridget. I shouldn't be a scrap surprised if you had."

Bridget stared open-mouthed.

"You poor thing!" she said, after a pause. "You ain't a bit fit to earn your own living."

"No; I am not," said Florence; but here a ghost of a smile crossed her face.

Bridget after a time went out of the room. Florence did not feel at all inclined to eat the dry ham and stale bread, which were all that was left for her breakfast. She had a certain sense of the great injustice of being treated in this manner; for was not Mr Timmins paying Mrs Fortescue just as much for her support as though she and her sister were both living with the good lady?

After a time, she got up and left the dining-room. Things were very dreary. It was so strange of Mrs Fortescue to go out. Mrs Fortescue had always fussed a good deal about the girls, and had made their arrangements for the day her first consideration. Now she did not seem to think Florence of the slightest importance, and had gone away without alluding to her. She had not come back either. Florence felt restless. She wanted to go and see Susie Arbuthnot, but thought it was too early. She left the room, however, prepared to put on her outdoor things. She would have liked it if Michael had called. Now was the opportunity for Michael to show his devotion, to assure her of the great truth of his own words; then if she were as poor as a church mouse, she would still be all the world to him.

But Michael did not come. Florence ran up to her room. She put on her hat and jacket. They were just as becoming as yesterday, and her young face looked just as pretty—prettier, indeed; for sorrow had brought out fresh charms and had added to her loveliness. Her eyes, always bright and capable of varying expressions, were now filled with intense pathos.

She had just run downstairs, and was crossing the hall, when she saw Mrs Fortescue come in. To her relief, she perceived that this good woman was accompanied by Susie Arbuthnot.

"Oh Florence—dear!" said Susie.

She went straight up to the girl, folded her arms round her and kissed her.

"I have a proposal to make to you," she continued, "and if it is agreeable, we will carry it out at once. I don't think Mrs Fortescue will object, will you, Mrs Fortescue?"

"Well, really!" said Mrs Fortescue; "I don't think that *my* wishes are worth consulting. I am of no importance—no importance whatever. But all I insist upon is that until the twentieth of the month I receive the ten guineas a week which Mr Timmins owes for you and your sister. You are welcome to stay at my house, or to do what Susie Arbuthnot—who is quite extraordinary and unlike other people—proposes. But I will have my ten guineas a week, or I go to law with Mr Timmins. I will at least have that much money at my disposal."

"What do you want me to do, Susie?" said Florence, with that new-born dignity which suited her so very well, and with that wonderful, new pathos in her eyes which made her look altogether lovely.

"I want you to do this," said Susie; "to come straight back with me to the Grange. Neither father nor I want ten guineas, nor one penny a week, and you are to stay as long as ever you like. I want you to come now. Why, Flo, it is you I love just for yourself, not because you are an heiress. As a rule, I hate heiresses—not that I have met many."

"Nor have I," said Mrs Fortescue, with a snap. "They are mostly creatures of imagination. They don't exist outside story-books. Well, Florence, say what you will do. Of course you can stay here if you wish; I want you clearly to understand that I don't turn you out."

"Of course you don't," said Florence; "and I know that you will get your money in full. I'll see to that. But I should love to go with you, Susie; and—may I go at once?"

"Indeed you may, darling. I have come for you," said Susie Arbuthnot.

"Who will pack her things?" said Mrs Fortescue. "Bridget has no time to spare; when a woman is as poor as I am and has only one servant, she can't have that servant's time being given up doing odds and ends for penniless girls. Penniless girls ought to understand how to manage their own affaire; otherwise, they are no use in the world."

"Hush!" said Susie, in so stern a voice that Mrs Fortescue turned and looked at her in some amazement. "You will be sorry another time that you spoke like this. Come upstairs with me, Florence; we will soon put your things into their trunks, and then we can drive to the Grange. I will order a fly."

"I can pay for it, you know, Susie," said poor Florence. "I have plenty of money, plenty, until the twentieth of January—"

"And after that, nothing—nothing at all," said Mrs Fortescue. "Did ever any one before in all the world hear of such improvidence—girls who have had hundreds a year spent on them to be brought down to nothing! Oh, I have been shamefully deceived! But you'll rue it—both of you. Yes, you will. That sister of yours, Florence, is just as improvident as you are, and has just as little power of making herself useful to any one. This fine woman. Lady Marian Dixie, will soon discover her uselessness. But go upstairs, my dear, do. I shall be very glad to have your room. I cannot afford, however, to give you any of Bridget's valuable time."

Florence ran upstairs as if in a dream. Susie accompanied her.

"Don't fret, Florence," she said, when they entered the pretty bedroom. "She is a very hardened, money-loving woman, and you have managed to disappoint her; but she will get over this, of course."

"And you are not disappointed?" said Florence.

"Oh no, darling," said Susie with a smile. "I never in the very least cared about your money. It was you I loved, and you are not changed."

Here she took the bright girl's face between both her hands and kissed her on her lips.

"Oh, Florence!" she said. "Talk of *you* as penniless—you, with those eyes, that youth, that beauty and that true heart! Florence, darling; you are rich in great possessions!"

"I think I am," said Florence, joyfully, "now that I have found a friend. Oh yes," she added, "I am sure I am."

It took but a short time to pack the different articles of Florence's wardrobe into the neat trunks which were waiting to receive them. Susie herself went out to fetch a cab, and before lunch time Florence was installed at the Grange. The Colonel was delighted to see her, and received her with the same graceful old-fashioned courtesy he had done on Christmas Day. This was perhaps, if anything, slightly accentuated. He did not once allude to the subject of money, nor did he express any commiseration for Florence's poverty. On the contrary, he expected her to be in an excellent humour, and took her about the garden showing her his favourite plants, and pointing out different mysterious little plots of ground which would, as he expressed it, "blossom like the rose" when the spring arrived.

"Ah," he said, "it is a great mystery—a very, very great mystery, that of death and resurrection. All the seeds in the ground down there are apparently dead, and there is nothing as far as we can tell to call them into life again. Frost night after night, snow on the ground, biting cold rains, no growth, no movement—and yet the germ is safe within, folded in each of the little seeds; and when the right moment comes, it will begin to fructify, and there will come out the little tender plants— just the merest little shoots at first—which will grow together day by day; and then there will come the hardy plant, and then the bud, and then the blossom, and then again the seed; and that same must die in order to bring forth fresh life. It is all lovely and all true and like our own life, isn't it, Florence?"

"Yes," said Florence; "it does seem so."

"You are lonely without your sister, my dear."

"I am rather lonely," said Florence. But it was not the thought of Brenda which was depressing her. She had got over her separation from her sister for the time being: besides, they could meet, and would meet, at any time. She was expecting Michael Reid and wondering if he would look in at the Arbuthnots'. So far he had not come, nor had his name been alluded to.

While Florence and the old Colonel were pottering about the garden, out came Susie with her red and yet sunshiny face.

"Now," she said, "you two have talked long enough, and I want Florence. Florence, we are going to do a lot of preserving this afternoon. I mean to make more marmalade than I have ever made before, and it is a tremendous business; but I have managed to get a hundred Seville oranges at quite a moderate price at Johnson's. We'll begin our preparations as soon as ever lunch is over. But now it is on the table; so do come in, good folks, both of you, and eat."

"I should like to help with the marmalade too," said the Colonel.

Susie laughed.

"Oh no, you won't," she said. "You did last year, don't you remember? and nobody would eat the Colonel's marmalade. Each jar had to be marked 'Colonel Arbuthnot' on account of the thickness of the rinds. You had it all to yourself, and I think you are about sick of it."

"But I'll do better this time; I really will, Susie," said the poor Colonel.

"Oh, it does seem so very silly to cut up that beautiful rind so thick; it isn't men's work," said Susie, "and that's the truth; but it's meant for women like Florence and me. If Flo cuts the rinds thick, she will feel the full impetus of my wrath. You go into the library and get your books in order, father. I dare say Flo and I will come in and read to you presently; but between lunch and tea-time we are going to be busy over our marmalade, and we don't want you hovering round."

"There, there!" said the Colonel, "there, there! What is the good of an old man who is always in the way?"

"Things are being done for him all the time," said Susie. "Now, how do you like that curry, sir? Let me tell you that I made it myself."

"It is delicious, my dear," said the Colonel. "I could almost fancy myself back in Bengal. It has got the true oriental flavour. Where did you discover that knack of blending the ingredients so that you don't get one flavour over and above the others? Really—this curry is a *chef-d'oeuvre*. Try some, won't you, Florence?"

But Florence declared that she could not eat curry with the true eastern flavour and preferred some cold mutton, which Susie out for her with right good-will.

"I like your food," she said. "It is so good and wholesome. I hate messy things. Mrs Fortescue was always making things up for us, imagining that we could not eat plain things."

"You will get very plain things here," said Susie. "It's only father who has to be petted and fussed over. But then he is worth it—he is such an old dear," and she looked at him with her honest eyes beaming with affection.

When the meal had come to an end, Florence and Susie were immediately supplied with two large linen aprons, and the work of making marmalade began. For a time, Florence pretended to enjoy it, then her knife slackened, and Susie shouted to her that her pieces of orange peel were almost if not quite worthy of the Colonel's own.

"I am not going to have it," she said. "We can only manage to live comfortably by never wasting anything, and if you can't cut the oranges better than that, you had better stop."

"Oh, Susie, I am sorry! I will be good." Florence made a violent effort to do better, but ended in cutting her finger, and then Susie had to spend a long time in binding up the wound and pitying the sufferer.

"You are not a bit yourself to-day," she said. "What is the matter with you?"

"Well, I don't know," said Florence. "I am both happy and unhappy."

"I shouldn't have thought," said Susie gravely, "that you were a bit the sort of girl to care whether you had money or not."

"I shouldn't mind in the least," answered Florence, "only that it seems to make such a wonderful difference with people. Mrs Fortescue has turned out so horribly nasty."

"Oh no," said Susie. "She is quite natural; she will be all right in a day or two, and as affectionate to you as ever. She is a little disappointed, that is all. She takes her disappointments badly: some people do."

"But you, Susie—you and your father—you are so sweet."

"Well, dear," said Susie, "I do trust that our sweetness does not depend on the fact that you and Brenda are entitled to so many hundreds a year. I have always been fond of you just for your two selves and for nothing else."

"There is one thing that makes me a little anxious," said Florence; "but, of course, it is all right—of course it is."

"What is it, darling?" asked Susie. "You may as well out with it, for I can see plainly that you are harbouring a very uncomfortable and anxious thought in your heart."

"Well," said Florence, "it is this way. I am thinking about Michael. I am wondering if—if he will mind."

"Do you mean Michael Reid?"

"Yes."

Susie was silent, but she laid down the sharp knife with which she had been cutting her orange peel and looked full at the girl.

"What do you think yourself, Florence?"

"I think this," said Florence. "I think that if I doubt him I am about the most unworthy, the most cowardly girl in all God's world. For when he told me—oh yes, Susie, he did tell me—for when he told me so plainly that he loved me, he said it was for myself, and that if I were as poor as a church mouse, he would love me just, just the same."

"Then, of course, it is all right," said Susie. She spoke cheerfully.

"Yes; of course it must be all right," said Florence; "but I knew at the time that I was poor, although I was not allowed to say a word about it.

Mr Timmins had given us such explicit directions, and Brenda and I felt ourselves in quite a false position. So I told him I would not give him his answer for a week. I shall probably know nothing about him for at least a week."

"Probably not," said Susie. "And now, let me give you a word of advice. I have known Michael since he was a boy. He is a good fellow, as young men go; but he has plenty of faults—"

"Oh no—I am sure he hasn't."

"He has," said Susie. "Every one has. You have, and I have, and even daddy has—particularly when it comes to cutting the orange peel. But now, I will tell you what I feel. If Michael finds when he is put to the test that he doesn't care for you, although you are as poor as a church mouse, you are very well rid of him; and if he does care for you, he is worth waiting for."

"Yes, yes," said Florence; "that is what I think. And oh, Susie, I mean to work so hard just to help to earn money for him."

"You poor little thing!" said Susie. "I wonder how you will earn money."

"I don't know; but there must be lots of ways. A girl can't be given hands, and arms, and legs, and a brain, and a head all for nothing."

"A great many are, it seems to me," said Susie, with a sigh. "But there —we have cut enough orange peel for to-day. We must go and get tea for daddy. Come with me into the kitchen, and I will complete your education by teaching you how to make a proper tea-cake."

Chapter Eleven.

Rich in Love.

As long as she lived, Florence Heathcote never forgot that week which she spent with the Arbuthnots. They belonged to that noble race of people who live for others. They were not rich—indeed, far from that, they were extremely poor. Had any one been told the exact extent of Colonel Arbuthnot's income, that person would have stared and refused to believe it. But then the person would not have known Susie's saving powers, her wonderful capability for making tenpence do the work of a shilling, for never losing a penny's worth in any transaction, and for renovating her old garments so that they looked almost like new. The money she was allowed for clothes she spent, as a rule, on other people. What did it matter if her hat was last year's fashion when poor Mrs Jones and Mary Bryce got their nourishing soup, and when the orphan child of that gallant fellow, William Engelhart, was taught by her to read and write, and she paid the necessary money for his small education? The fact was, fashionable hats, jackets, and skirts would not have become Susie in the very least: she would have looked absolutely out of place in them. No one ever looked at Susie Arbuthnot's clothes: the eye was arrested by the kindliness in the kindly face, by the smile round the good-natured lips, by the strength and firmness of purpose of that hand grip, by the noble soul that radiated from that somewhat homely countenance.

And if Susie was good and could do good, she was but her father's complement. Each seemed to complete the character. There never had been before, nor ever since, a father and daughter so wholly and completely one. They had the same tastes, the same desires. Life with them was a little season to be spent in the school of the Almighty. It was the will of God that they should learn His lessons, and they learned them with submission, with cheerfulness, and without a thought of grumbling. The books they liked best were books that spoke about a future state. Often on Sunday evenings they sat close together, talking of that period when they should lay down for ever this vile body, and put on the celestial body. But they were not morbid in their conversations. They were always simple, and homely and direct. It was their pleasure to do what little good they could. Every one loved them at Langdale, and they were the life and light of the place.

The Colonel was just as economical in the matter of clothes as Susie. That winter overcoat of his must have seen the light for long years— one might almost say, generations. Its original black had changed to a musty green, but at one time it had been cut by a fashionable tailor, and, somehow or other, the Colonel looked well in it. He was very upright, as all well-drilled men are, and he walked with a certain martial stride, holding his head erect, and looking all the world in the face. He was not ashamed of himself or of anybody else. He hated sin and wickedness, and smallnesses and the love of riches, and would fight against these things to his dying day. But he sincerely pitied those who had sinned and had repented. As to the poor of this world—those who were a little poorer than himself—he took them under his special protection.

"Dear me, Susie," he would say; "I think we might ask little Miss Hudson on a visit. The weather is so cold, and I am persuaded the little creature cannot afford a fire in her bedroom. It would never do to ask her the question, but while the intense cold lasts, it would be nice to have her here. She could go on teaching the Hibbert children, and come to us for her meals, and have the enjoyment of her snug little room with a bright fire in it in the evenings. I could fancy how she would luxuriate at the flicker of the firelight as she dropped asleep."

Susie acquiesced, of course, but Florence, who was present, said—

"That is all very well; but what is Miss Hudson to do when she leaves you, Colonel?"

"We'll keep her as long as the cold weather lasts," said the Colonel, rubbing his hands. "She can go back to her own rooms when the weather becomes mild. Run round to her early this morning, Susie, my love; and be sure you have something specially appetising for dinner."

Susie promised with that bright glance of hers and a smile which irradiated her face for a moment and then left it grave and practical. She meant to have a dinner of bones that day, and a bone dinner would not do for Miss Hudson. Florence had been initiated into the bone dinners, and they were really quite remarkable. They were so good that she quite enjoyed them; but they were never spoken about. They consisted of two or three pennyworth of bones, which were boiled down to make a strong soup, into which was introduced every known vegetable that Susie could lay her hands on out of the garden. No one ever spoke of the absence of meat on the day when the bone dinner appeared. Each person received a portion of bone with the rich gravy and vegetables, and it would have been considered very incorrect not to praise the delicious, tender repast. The Colonel as a rule said, "What good meat we get from our butcher," and Susie nodded, picking at her bone viciously as she did so, knowing quite well that she would not get one morsel of meat from it.

Florence had been told the mystery of the bone dinner.

"We have it sometimes three times a week," said Susie. "We need not have it at all, you know, but the price of the meat goes to certain very poor widows in the village. I could not manage to give it to them in any other way, and I cannot tell you what sustenance father and I get from our bones and vegetables. You will have the same, and you won't mind, will you, Florence?"

Florence was delighted, but rather overdid the occasion in the first instance of the bone dinner, declaring that the meat was almost too tender. But the Colonel gave her a keen glance which was almost stern, and she found herself colouring and was silent.

Now the day on which Miss Hudson was to be asked to go and stay with the Arbuthnots was a bone dinner day, and Susie was a little perplexed as to how to manage the matter. She consulted Florence on the subject. Florence was very much excited on her own account, for that was the very day of the week on which Michael Reid had promised to come to receive her answer. Nevertheless, Susie's anxious face drew her at once, and she said, after a pause—

"You could have some little special thing for her alone, couldn't you?"

"No; that would never do," said Susie, frowning. "She would not touch it. She would push the bones about in her plate, and make a noise with them, and pretend she was delighted, and the special thing would go out of the room, for not one of us would look at it. What is to be done?"

"I tell you what," said Florence, blushing very deeply. "I have got such a lot of money. May not I provide the dinner to-day? You have been, oh, so kind to me, so sweet, so angelic. Do, do, *do* let me! The darling Colonel won't notice, I know he won't. It will be just our secret. Why may not I have this pleasure?"

"There now," said Susie; "why, of course you may. Give me half-a-crown, and I will get something excellent for dinner."

So Florence broke into the first of her ten sovereigns, and Susie started off to market, determined to buy beef which should not be rivalled by any other beef that had ever been cooked before in the United Kingdom. When she had gone, Florence went away by herself.

She was afraid to go out; she did not care to stay still. She was restless and unhappy. Michael ought to have arrived. He knew quite well where she was, for she had met him once during the week, and had even told him that she was staying with the Arbuthnots. On this occasion the gallant lieutenant had been seen walking down the High Street with two or three young ladies. But he had stopped at sight of Florence looking so radiant, so different from any other girl, in her beautiful sealskin jacket with that becoming sealskin cap. He had looked at her, but had said nothing, cruelly contenting himself with taking off his hat. But his eyes—and Michael had very handsome eyes—seemed to express volumes, and Florence had gone back again to the Arbuthnots' house feeling warm and happy.

Yes; she knew now quite well that she loved him, and love was beautiful. She was not a poor girl, after all; she was rich, far richer than Brenda, far richer than Susie or the Colonel. In a short time she would be publicly engaged to Michael, and then would begin the delightful task of working for their future home. She had heard of girls who, when engaged, spoke of the bottom drawer in their room as containing treasures which they amassed for the time when they would be married. Florence would have her bottom drawer; and oh! how many and what beautiful things she would put into it!—a wealth of love, a world of devotion; courage, hope, steadfastness. She could scarcely believe her own heart: she was learning so much, oh, so much during that week she spent with the Arbuthnots.

For the first time in all her young life Florence did perceive how very little value money really was. It could not buy the great things of life. She had hitherto never thought about it at all. She had had it in abundance; it had been but to ask to obtain. When she wanted a pretty dress, it was given to her. When she wished for a trinket, it became her own. The best rooms at school were kept for Brenda and herself; the best seats at table were theirs. The headmistress made a fuss about them: the other teachers regarded them with affection, and spoke of them as they would of princesses. Florence supposed, and rightly, that this was because they were rich. In the holidays they had a really glorious time. Who could fuss more about them than Mrs Fortescue? What lovely lodgings she took for them at the seaside, paying more than one dared to think for the spacious rooms where they lived and looked out upon the sparkling waves. Once she had taken them to Paris, and they had had a truly glorious time.

Yes; nothing had been denied them up to the present. They had been urged to learn, too, just because it was such poor fun for rich girls to be ignorant. Rich girls ought to know things. They ought to be rich in mind as well as in body.

Well, Florence had done her best. She was a fairly clever girl. She had certain talents, and she had made the most of them. She was, of course, very young, but she felt, on the whole, rather old. This last week had made her old. She had learned a great deal during this week —the immense, the terrible difference between extreme poverty and extreme wealth. It never once occurred to her that Mr Timmins had behaved badly in not describing to them more accurately the true state of affaire. Brenda had not blamed him, nor did she. He had acted according to her father's will; and her dear father must have known what was beat. No one was to blame. They had had their good time— as far as wealth was concerned. But oh, how joyful! she had discovered something else: the wealth, the great wealth of love—love; which could exist in a poorly furnished house between an old man and a middle-aged woman; love, which could rejoice the hearts of those who were poorer than itself. And had she not also found her own true love? her lover, who cared for her just because she was herself, just because she was Florence Heathcote, a young girl with a heart to respond to his heart, a love to return for his love? Oh yes, she was happy!

The day of days had come. After Florence had given her half-crown to Susie Arbuthnot, she ran up to her room to prepare for her lover's visit. He was quite sure to come. He had promised to come to-day for her answer: and she had it ready. She had not put it on paper, she had folded it up inside her heart. It was waiting for him. She would open the door of her heart and just let him peep in and see what it was like— rosy, red, glorious with the tint of the morning; and his—all his!

As she entered the house, she was singing under her breath. She had a sweet voice, and her gay notes thrilled through the old house and brought the Colonel out of his study.

"Well, Florence," he said.

"Well, Colonel," she answered. She went up to him and took his hand. Then she said, looking full into his face: "I am so awfully happy!"

"I am glad of it, dear," he replied. "I am more than glad to find that there is a young girl in this world who has been brought up as you have been brought up, and who thinks nothing at all of riches. It takes most of us many long years to learn the lesson which you have learned at once."

"I am not thinking about riches at all," said Florence. She looked at him again, and then she resolved to tell. "May I come with you into your study for a few minutes?" she said.

"Why, certainly, my dear child," he replied; and he took her hand and led her into the study. He shut the door and turned and faced her.

"Well, Florence," he said; "what is it?"

"You say I am not rich, Colonel Arbuthnot," was Florence's answer; "but I am just about as rich as any girl can be."

She blushed, and her beautiful eyes grew bright—bright with that sort of look which made it impossible to tell what their colour was, only there seemed to be a great deal of gold about them—a sort of golden brown. Then she dropped her long, black lashes, and her face, which had been so rosy, grew pale. She lifted her eyes again, and fixed them on the Colonel's face.

"He is coming to-day," she said; "that is why I am happy. He may be here at any hour—at any minute. I am most awfully happy. A week ago I was astonished when he said what he did say; but now I am just happy. I am very rich, Colonel, because he loves me so much."

"Who in the world is the girl talking about?" said the Colonel, for he at least knew nothing about Florence's attachment.

Florence looked at him half shyly.

"Can't you guess?" she said. "Didn't you see us together on Christmas Day?" But the Colonel still looked puzzled. A good many people had dined in their hospitable house on Christmas Day, and he had not particularly noticed either Brenda or Florence at that time.

"You must explain a little more, dear," he said very gently.

"Well," said Florence, "I will tell you, for you will know all about it very, very soon. It is Michael—Michael Reid."

"What?" said the Colonel.

"We have been friends always, but I never guessed—in fact, I have never had the smallest idea that he—he cared for me; I did not think about those sorts of things; but on Christmas Day he did seem a little different from other men, and the next day we took a walk—a long walk—and he told me—oh, that is what makes it so beautiful!—that he loved me just, just for myself alone."

The Colonel looked rather uneasy.

"Michael Reid!" he said. "Of course I know the lad, I have known him since he was a boy. He is not well off, Florence."

"That is just it," said Florence. "That is the beautiful part. We neither of us care twopence whether he is well off or not. He says that he would love me if I were as poor as a church mouse, and I feel just the same for him. We are very rich, both of us, because we love each other so much. That is about it, Colonel. How can you call me a poor girl, when I am so rich in love?"

"God grant it, my darling! God grant that you are," said the Colonel in a reverent tone. Then, bending over her, he kissed her on her white forehead. "You have no father living, so I must take his place for the time being," he added.

"Michael is coming to see me to-day," said Florence. "He may be here any minute. I want to put on my very prettiest frock for him. There is nothing one would not do for the man who loves you, is there?"

"Nothing, nothing, of course," said the Colonel.

Very soon afterwards Florence left the room. As she was going away, the Colonel said—

"I must see about this: I must be a father to you; I feel that I stand in the place of a father to you at the present moment."

"Oh, how sweet you are!" said Florence. "He will be here himself—any minute; for the week is up to-day, and he is coming to get my answer. He knows all, all about my being poor, and he is coming to-day for my answer. I must go upstairs now to make myself look my very best for him."

She went away, closing the door very softly behind her. The Colonel heard her singing as she ran upstairs. He then sank heavily into his accustomed armchair. He rested his elbows on the arms of the chair and gazed straight before him with a deep frown between his brows. In truth, he was more troubled than he had ever been before.

After a long time, during which he had been thinking deeply, he went to his desk and wrote a short note to Susie.

"Dear Susie,—
"I may not be in to lunch. Don't wait for me.
"Your loving,—
"Father."

He then put on his greatcoat, that shabby coat which had grown green with age, took up his hat and gold-headed stick, and marched out into the little street of Langdale. The Colonel had never looked fiercer, nor yet more dignified than he did now. His moustaches had taken quite a formidable military curl. His white hair was white as snow, but his black brows, and the gleam in his eyes under them, made him look quite a remarkable and imposing figure. One or two people spoke to him, but he did not answer. They wondered afterwards what was the matter with Colonel Arbuthnot. He was certainly very upright. He was an amazing figure for a man of his age—so the women said who watched him from their cottage doors. He was bent on something, just as bent as he had been when he was young and was fighting the battles of his country.

He went straight to Mrs Fortescue's house. He rang the bell, and when Bridget answered his summons, he said—

"You needn't tell me that your mistress is at home, because I see her in her dining-room window. I want to say something to her." Then Bridget made way for him, and he went into Mrs Fortescue's presence uninvited.

Chapter Twelve.

Tried and Found Wanting.

Mrs Fortescue was busily engaged answering letters which had come to her owing to an advertisement which she had put into *The Times* and other daily papers to the effect that she wished to mother young orphan girls to whom she could give undying care and devotion. She was emphasising these special qualities in her replies, and looked up with decided annoyance and a frown between her brows when Colonel Arbuthnot appeared. One glance at him, however, caused her manner to change. She by no means wished to make an enemy of the Colonel; although he was poor—never for a moment pretending to be anything else—he was quite the most respected person in the whole of Langdale. He was influential, too, and his name as one of her late Majesty's most esteemed soldiers would carry weight in any circle. She wanted to secure him as a reference, and was therefore very mild and gentle when she stood up to give him her cordial greeting.

"Sit down, Colonel; do sit down," she said. "I am so glad to see you. How very fortunate that I was not out. I told Bridget to say that I could not be disturbed this morning, for I am specially engaged; but never to you, dear Colonel; never to you."

The Colonel made no response of any sort. He sat and stared moodily at Mrs Fortescue. Mrs Fortescue was puzzled at the expression on his face.

"And how is my dear child?" she said. "You know I call both the dear Heathcote girls my children. They have been as children to me for many years now, and ah! how fondly I have tried to act a mother's part to both of them, God alone can tell."

"If I were you, madam," said the Colonel somewhat severely, "I would leave the name of the Almighty out of this business. There are times and seasons for everything, and this, in my opinion, is not the time to speak of God, except, indeed, to beg for His forgiveness, which all we poor sinners need—all, all of us."

The Colonel's voice changed as he uttered the last words, but only for an instant. Once again his black brows came beetling down over his eyes, and once more he looked like one ready to fight to the death in a losing cause. Mrs Fortescue was not, however, a woman possessed of any insight to character. She was as essentially worldly minded as

Colonel Arbuthnot was the reverse.

"How is my Florence?" she repeated.

"Florence Heathcote is well, thank you."

"It was so noble of you to take her into your house as you have done," said Mrs Fortescue. "Few in your circumstances would have done it. It was just the very thing for the dear child—a sort of stepping stone for her, in fact, to—"

"To what?" asked the Colonel.

His tone slightly startled Mrs Fortescue.

"To her future life, my dear friend. Alack and alas! to think that those poor children should be the sport of poverty. How cruel was their father's will! How much, much more sensible it would have been to send them both to a charity school, and keep the little money for their needs when they grew up, that has been lavishly wasted year after year on their education. I have been counting carefully, and I make not the least doubt—"

"Excuse me," said the Colonel: "I have come just to ask you a question and then to leave you. I am somewhat busy, and have not a moment to spare. Did you, or did you not, Mrs Fortescue—"

"Why, what is it?" asked Mrs Fortescue. "What a severe tone you are taking, my dear Colonel—and we have been such old friends."

"*Will you listen*?" said the Colonel, and he thumped his hand on the table with such force that one of the letters which Mrs Fortescue was answering dropped on the floor.

"Of course I will listen," she said gently. "Do calm yourself, dear Colonel. What can be wrong?"

"Nothing; at least, I hope nothing. I simply want to ask you one question, and I am then going."

"Of course I will answer it."

"Did you let Major Reid and his son know the change with regard to Florence Heathcote's fortune?"

Now this was about the very last question which Mrs Fortescue expected to be asked. She changed colour and turned rather white.

"I—" she began.

"I see you did," said the Colonel. "It doesn't matter in the least—on the contrary, I regard it as a good thing, an excellent thing. Good-morning: I won't keep you another moment."

"But—really, Colonel—you are so strange—"

Mrs Fortescue spoke to empty air. The Colonel had left her. He stood for a minute or two in the street, pondering. He was making up his mind whether he would himself go straight to see Major Reid or leave things alone. While he was so deliberating in his mind, he saw Michael Reid coming down the street. Michael's well-groomed figure, his dainty dress, his spotless turn-out, the very way he twirled his cane, the very manner in which he smoked his cigar irritated the Colonel almost past bearing.

"Insolent puppy!" he said to himself. He crossed the street, however, and went straight up to the young man.

"I presume you are on your way to my house?"

"Well, I—ar—I did not intend to call this morning," said Reid, turning red as he spoke.

The Colonel gave him a shrewd glance.

"Florence Heathcote is expecting you. When I was young, it was considered extremely ungallant to keep young ladies waiting. We may as well walk together. What a pleasant morning, isn't it, for the time of year?"

Reid murmured something. He wondered how he could possibly escape the Colonel. He did not wish to displease him, and yet he certainly had no desire to see Florence on that special morning. While he was deliberating, the Colonel stole his hand inside the young man's arm.

"We are old friends, aren't we, Michael?" he said. "I have known you from your birth. I am exceedingly glad to hear that you have formed an attachment to so excellent a girl as Florence. Now, my dear fellow, pray don't blush: who minds the words of an old soldier like myself? I was young once: I loved once. My Susie's mother and I married when we were very poor. But, God knows! there never was a happier union. The only sad thing about it—the only sad thing was, its brevity. God took my angel to Himself. But he left me Susie, and I am the last to complain. There's nothing, my dear young fellow, like roughing it a bit in the early years of marriage, provided, of course, there is true love; and you, Michael, could not be such a dog as to pretend to love a woman when you do not love her all the time. Ah—and here we are.

See Florence; she has noticed us. A sweet girl, Michael—a sweet girl. I can see you afterwards, that is, if you wish it. I stand in the position of a father to Florence, for the time being, her own father having left us—gone to join the majority—ah, what a majority it is! Now you go right in. You will find her all alone. The best girl in the world, true as steel, afraid of nothing. God bless you, Michael."

Certainly Michael Reid had not the faintest idea when he started on his walk that morning of going near the Grange. He knew perfectly well, however, that it was the day when Florence was prepared to give him her answer. He was uncomfortably aware of the fact. It had stayed with him in his dreams on the previous night, and disturbed him a good deal. He knew all about the Heathcotes' reverse of fortune—that was how his father chose to express it. The girls were, his father said, a pair of impostors. They had been palmed off on the people as heiresses. They did not own a penny in the world. As to their good looks—Brenda was, if anything, a plain girl, and Florence was just moderately good-looking. Of course, Michael must never give her a thought again.

The Major had urged his son to leave Langdale; but something, he could not tell what, kept Michael on the spot. He wanted to see Florence once more, and yet he dreaded seeing her inexpressibly. Well, now he was caught—fairly caught by Colonel Arbuthnot, dragged to the house against his will. What a position for a man, a man who was terribly in debt and who required all the assistance that a rich wife could give him. Surely rich wives were to be had, although they might not be as taking as pretty Florence. There was no help for it, however; he could not possibly marry her. He had absolutely forgotten that remark of his, that he would love her and make her his wife if she was as poor as a church mouse.

Florence had put on her very prettiest frock, and Florence's prettiest frock was one to wonder at, for it was made by a dressmaker who was also an artist; it was somewhat the colour of an autumn leaf—seeming to shade away from her dear and radiant complexion; and her sunny brown hair seeming to add to the glories in her brown eyes (oh, how brown they were this morning!), and to bring out the bewitching sparkles of her face.

When Michael entered the room, Florence ran up to him joyfully.

"So you have come!" she said. "I was expecting you. Sit down, won't you? How are you, Michael?"

She looked at him with a certain pathos in her pretty eyes. He came eagerly to her. He could not help himself. He forgot, just for a minute or two, that she was a penniless girl; she looked so radiant, so different from anybody else.

"Oh, Florence!" he said.

She clasped both his hands, holding them tightly and standing close to him.

"I know, dear," she said, "I know you are sorry for me. But I am not one to be sorry for myself: I am not really, Mike. You have heard, of course, that Brenda and I, instead of being rich, are poor. But that doesn't matter. At first I thought perhaps it did a little. I knew, of course, darling, it would never matter with you after what you said. You remember what you said, don't you, Mike?"

"What—what was it?" said the young man.

"That you would love me all the same, and marry me all the same if I were as poor as—as a church mouse? Do you know that at the time I absolutely knew that I was as poor as a church mouse?"

"And you never told me?" he said, trying to let go her hands and yet feeling attracted by her as he had never been attracted before.

"I was not allowed to," she answered. "Mr Timmins had enjoined Brenda and me not to breathe a word of it to any one until he thought it best that the secret should be known."

"Everybody knows it now—my father and every one," said Michael; and his voice was very gloomy.

"But it doesn't matter a scrap," she answered. "You don't think I mind? Why, you know in some ways it makes it far more exciting; and I will tell you one of the ways, Michael. It makes me so sure and certain that you love me, not for my money, but for myself. It would be perfectly awful for a girl to marry a man just because he liked her money and did not care for herself." Michael Reid winced. "But you are not like that, darling, and if you want me—why, here—here I am. I made up my mind fully a day or two ago. It is all right; I am quite willing to be poor with you. I know we can't be married for a little, but that doesn't matter. I am going to work ever so hard: we'll both work, won't we, darling Michael? We'll do our very best, and I know we'll win in the end. I don't mind being engaged at all, even if it's for a long time."

"Florence," said Michael.

He dropped his hands to his sides and looked full at the girl.

"What is it?" she asked, a queer expression darkening her eyes. She stepped a little away from him.

"I must write to you, dear," he said. "I—I will explain things by letter. You are good to me—very, very good—but I will explain things by letter."

"But—Michael, can't you speak? Don't you—don't you—really love me?"

"Of course I do—of course I do—"

Just then the door was opened, and in came Colonel Arbuthnot.

"I am sorry to interrupt you two young people," he said, "but the fact is, I want to hear what arrangements you have made. I stand in the place of father to this young girl, Michael Reid. Are you willing to be her husband; to wait for her until you can afford to marry; to live a clean and good life for her sake, sir; to make yourself worthy of her? She is a very precious gem, sir—a girl hard to match: she has purity of heart and honesty of motive. She is innocent, sir, as the dawn, and beautiful, sir, as the sunrise. Do you think you are fit for her? Tell me so, honestly, and at once: otherwise, I shall not be able to give my consent."

"I am not—I am not fit for her; I am not worthy," said Michael.

"That is for yourself to decide, of course—"

"Oh—but Michael—" said poor Florence.

"Florence, dear, be silent. Michael Reid must speak now from his full heart. Michael, I know all about this little affair."

"*Little* affair!" said Florence. She felt indignant at the word "little" being introduced. The Colonel turned to her with a very gentle smile. He laid his hand on her arm.

"You are very young, my darling," he said; "only a child—little more than a child. You don't understand the world at all."

"He said he wanted me for myself; that—that he would love me if I were as poor as a church mouse," said Florence.

"You did say those words, didn't you, Michael Reid?" said the Colonel.

Michael dropped his eyes.

"One says a great many things," was his reply, "that one—doesn't—"

"Ah, I see," said the Colonel. "You thought Florence Heathcote would be rich. Florence, don't leave the room,"—for Florence was moving towards the door—"I wish you to stay, my dear. There is a little lesson which you two young people must learn, and you must learn it now, and in my presence. It will hurt you both for a time, but in the end you will both recover. Now, Michael, you made love to Florence Heathcote, believing her to be well off."

"Everybody else thought the same," said Michael Reid.

"Then you didn't mean that about the church mouse?" said Florence.

"To tell the truth," said Michael, desperately, "it was quite impossible—I mean, it *is* quite impossible. I am not at all well off myself—"

"But I said I was willing to wait," said Florence.

"*Let him* speak, Florence; don't interrupt," said the Colonel.

"There is no use in a long engagement," said Reid. "I am exceedingly sorry—I cannot pretend that I am in a position to marry a penniless girl. I—I have debts; I am desperately sorry—I would have written—I ought to have written—I have been a fearful coward, but—"

"Then you resign all claim to Florence Heathcote's hand?" said Colonel Arbuthnot.

"Yes; I am obliged to; I am terribly, terribly sorry; it is fearfully bad of me." Michael raised his eyes, met the flashing ones of Florence, then lowered them again. She was quite still for a minute. All the colour had gone out of her face. She was only eighteen; but a girl's first love is sacred, and something was burned and withered, never to be restored again, in her young heart at that moment. She went straight up to Michael Reid.

"You didn't mean a word that you said. You deceived me that day when we walked home by the river."

"I didn't mean to," he said in a shamefaced way.

"Well, it is at an end," said Colonel Arbuthnot. "There is no use in prolonging this scene. After all, Florence, you are years and years too young to be married; and as to you, Reid, you are not in any way worthy of Florence Heathcote. Some day, I trust, my dear child, you will find a man to love you for yourself, who will not think of your money, but of you."

"My money?" said Florence. "I have no money."

"That is not the point at present," said Colonel Arbuthnot. "The point is that you have discovered—as many another girl does—that you have loved some one who is unworthy of you. I don't say that you are all bad, Reid, I hope you are very far from it; but when you and your father schemed to secure this young girl simply because she was, as you imagined, rich, you overshot the mark, sir, both of you, understand me, you overshot the mark. And now I shall have the pleasure of showing you the door, Michael Reid. While Florence is here, you don't enter my house—no, sir; you don't enter it. Go, sir; go at once."

It was impossible, under such circumstances, even for a lieutenant in His Majesty's army to make a graceful exit, and Michael Reid looked uncommonly like a beaten hound as he went out of the house. As to Florence, she did not glance at either the Colonel or Michael, but rushed up to her room. There she bolted the door and flung herself on her bed.

Chapter Thirteen.

Lady Marian Explains.

Whether she was weak or not, whether she was angry or indifferent, Florence Heathcote shed very few tears. She came downstairs in that frock which was so like the colour of a rich autumn leaf. She partook of lunch with the Colonel and Susie, and afterwards went into the kitchen with Susie in order to prepare as good a dinner as possible for Miss Hudson.

Whenever Susie spoke to her, she laughed. Susie wondered if she felt anything. It was not until that evening that any of Florence's real feelings came out.

It was late in the evening when something very unexpected happened. No less a person than Brenda appeared on the scene. She had come down from London by the last train and come straight to the Arbuthnots' house by the invitation of the Colonel and Susie. They had said nothing to Florence on the subject. Florence had indeed gone up to bed. She expected to spend the whole night in those transports of grief which the overthrow of all hopes must induce. But somehow, when she saw Brenda, the tears were dry in her eyes, and a feeling of lightness visited her heart.

"Oh, Brenda, darling!" she said. "Why ever have you come? Did Lady Marian Dixie allow you to visit me so soon? How perfectly sweet of her!"

"Mr Timmins has brought me," said Brenda. "He had a telegram in the course of the morning from Colonel Arbuthnot, and came to see me, and has brought me down. I don't quite understand what it all means; but he is talking to Colonel Arbuthnot now, and you and I are to share that little bed, Flo. Do you mind, just for one night?"

"It's all over between Mike and me," said Florence. "Did you know that, Brenda?"

"Oh, you poor, poor darling!" said Brenda.

"But he said—"

"Yes, he said," interrupted Florence—and her tone was one of scorn —"but he didn't mean it—he was put to the proof to-day—and—he didn't mean a word of it. He wanted my money, not me. Oh—don't let's talk about him! I'd have got engaged to him; I had made up my mind to, and I—I'd have loved him—yes—most truly I'd have loved him—and waited for him—oh! years and years, and worked and worked to save money for him. But he didn't want it; he didn't want poor little me at all. Oh, how I hate all men, Brenda!" Brenda flung her arms round her sister's neck and kissed her many times.

"I have got you," said Florence; "we'll work together somehow. If I had been engaged, it would in a sort of way have divided us."

"It would certainly," said Brenda; "that is quite true."

"It is lovely to be close to you," said Florence; "and you look happier than ever. Oh! I should have had a perfectly awful time since I parted from you if it had not been for the dear Arbuthnots. I never knew any one like Mrs Fortescue; she was so angry when she found we had no money that she wouldn't even give me eggs for my breakfast; I had nothing but a little bit from that ham bone. Don't you remember that ham bone, Brenda?"

"Yes," said Brenda. "I remember Bridget told me how sick she was of it, how she had to make her dinner from it almost every day."

"As far as I can tell, I dare say she is still making her dinner from it," said Florence. "But anyhow, I told you in my letter, didn't I? how dear, darling Susie came and brought me away to stay here. I have been here for a week—I mean newly a week; and oh! I have been so happy —that is, until to-day. I have been finding out that money means nothing at all. No one who lived in the house with the Arbuthnots would think anything at all about money; for they are poor, but they never make a fuss. They manage on so little, and they give away every penny they can to those who are still poorer than themselves. But to-day has been awful—quite, quite awful!"

"You mean about Michael Reid?"

"Oh yes: I don't think I can ever be the same girl again."

"Do you know," said Brenda, "when Mr Timmins and I arrived at the station this evening, we saw Michael in the distance. Michael was going away with a lot of luggage and the Major was with him; he was saying good-bye to him. I don't think Michael saw me."

"Don't speak of him; I hate him even to be spoken about!" said Florence.

"He was subjected to a test," said Brenda, "and he certainly did not stand the ordeal. Well, you and I will do the best we can; and I

114

somehow think we'll be happy together."

"How does Lady Marian treat you? You look awfully well, Brenda," said Florence.

"Yes, I am well, and if it were not for you and that terrible Michael, I would be quite happy. I never could know, as Lady Marian's guest, that I was not as rich as ever. She has bought me lots of new things, and whenever she gets me anything, she gets the same for you. It is really quite ridiculous; I told her so. But her only remark was that our figures were the same and that it saved a lot of trouble. You will find almost a trousseau of clothes waiting for you when you come up to town to-morrow."

"Oh, I don't want them; I hate finery," said Florence.

"It would hurt Lady Marian very much indeed if we didn't accept her presents," said Brenda. "She wants to talk to us to-morrow about our future, and we are going back to town, both of us, by an early train with Mr Timmins."

"Oh," said Florence, "must we leave the dear Arbuthnots?"

"I have no doubt they will ask you to visit them sometimes in the holidays," said Brenda. "But we are going back to town, both of us, to-morrow, because Lady Marian particularly wants to see us."

After this conversation, the girls undressed and got into bed. Notwithstanding her grief, and the soreness at her heart, Florence slept soundly. In her sleep she had a dream that Michael Reid was at her feet, that he had repented of his pusillanimity of the day before, and was offering her once again his heart and hand, but that now she was refusing them with great scorn. She awoke from her dream to find her cheeks wet with tears and saw Susie looking down at her and smiling.

"I am so very sorry to wake you, Florence," she said, "but the fact is, you and Brenda must get up at once in order to catch the train. I've got a lovely breakfast ready for you both downstairs—real fresh eggs and broiled ham."

"Oh—but so expensive!" said Florence.

"I managed splendidly out of the money you gave me yesterday," said Susie. "You know what a delicious dinner we had, and how Miss Hudson did enjoy it. Well, there was enough over to make this good breakfast. And now you must hurry down, both of you, to eat it."

Florence sprang to her feet.

"I don't mind poverty, after all," she said, "if only I could spend it with you, Susie, and with your father."

"You shall come back to us, and whenever you come, you shall have a welcome—the best in all the world," said Susie. "And oh! do, my dear Florence, remember, when you are making orange marmalade that you cut the peel thin enough!"

"Yes, yes," said Florence. "But I don't think somehow," she added, with a dash of her old spirit, "that making orange marmalade is my *métier.*"

The girls dressed and went downstairs. The Colonel was waiting to receive them. Miss Hudson had had her breakfast and gone off to her pupils. The new-laid eggs were duly appreciated. The ham was pronounced delicious.

Presently, a cab came to the door and Brenda and Florence got in. Mr Timmins was to meet them at the railway station. The Colonel took both their hands as they were leaving.

"Good-bye, my dears," he said. "God bless you both. From what Mr Timmins tells me, I think you will be able to manage in the future; but if ever in any possible way you need a friend, you have but to remember me, who would love you both, my dear girls, were you as poor as the proverbial church mouse. And now, may a father have his privilege?"

He kissed each girl on her forehead, wrung their hands, and put them into the cab. As to Susie, she was wiping the tears from her eyes. The cab started on its way to the railway station and the pretty brown house disappeared from view. The different inhabitants of Langdale, who had known the girls in their wealth, saw them as they went by. Mrs Fortescue's Bridget was so much excited that she opened one of the bedroom windows and shrieked out—

"God bless you both, darlings!" But Mrs Fortescue only gazed at them severely from behind a wire blind.

She was thinking that there would be a good riddance at Langdale, and was comfortably feeling her purse, which was heavy with some money which Mr Timmins had paid her in person on the previous night. Yes, she had got rid of the Heathcotes; she must now find other girls to devote herself to with all a mother's care.

Bridget entered the room with her mistress' breakfast.

"Did you see the young ladies, madam?" she asked.

"What young ladies?" asked Mrs Fortescue.

"*Our* young ladies, madam—the Misses Heathcote. They've gone, both of them, poor darlings!"

"It's a very good thing they have gone," said Mrs Fortescue, in a severe voice. "They were quite nice girls, but were unfortunately brought up to deceive other people. They are now going to begin the battle of life in earnest, and I, for my part, am glad of it. They have plenty of faults, and will, I fear, find the lessons of life hard to learn."

"Oh, madam," said Bridget, "I never saw any one so good-natured as Miss Florence was about that ham bone—"

"That will do," said her mistress. "I expect," she added, "other young ladies to come and stay with me before long, and trust that you will exert yourself to cook well and to look after their interests."

"I was going to say, madam," said Bridget demurely, "that now that Miss Florence and Miss Brenda have gone, I should wish to give a month's notice."

Mrs Fortescue stared at her elderly servant. "What *do* you mean?" she said. "Give me your reasons."

"Well, madam, to tell you the truth—I don't like treating ladies, just because they ain't as rich as one expected them to be, with ham bones for breakfast. You will get some one else to help you when the new ladies come, madam," and Bridget flounced out of the room.

Meanwhile, Mr Timmins met the girls at the station. He took them up to town first-class and treated them with great respect and consideration. Florence could not help whispering to Brenda—

"Seeing that we are so very poor, it does seem absurd that we should always travel first-class."

"It's Mr Timmins' way," said Brenda. "I don't think he'd like," she added, "Lady Marian to know that we travelled in any other way."

"Well, we shall have to in the future," said Florence; "and," she added, "as far as I am concerned, I think it is almost more exciting to be poor. It is so delightful to manage. You can't imagine, Brenda, what fun Susie and I had contriving the dinners, more particularly the bone dinners."

"What *are* you talking about, children?" said Mr Timmins, waking up from a nap in which he had temporarily indulged.

Florence went and sat by his side and told him the story of the bone dinner.

"They are so delicious!" she said. "I never enjoyed anything more."

Mr Timmins seemed much interested in the story.

"'Pon my word!" he said; "if that is not about the very highest form of charity I have ever heard of. He that giveth to the poor lendeth to the Lord. It's a mighty good security, young ladies, mighty good. No fear of that security coming to smash."

Then he returned to his sheet of *The Times*, and did not speak again until the journey came to an end. When it did, Mr Timmins' own brougham was waiting for them. They got in, and drove straight to Lady Marian Dixie's house in Cadogan Place. Brenda seemed quite at home there, but Florence felt a little shy.

"Now," said Mr Timmins, "I will say goodbye to you both. Lady Marian has something to say to you, and if you want to see me later on in the day, you have but to telephone, and I will be with you. But I think Lady Marian would rather see you by herself."

"Come, Flo, come," said Brenda. "Oh, she is such a darling; you will love her soon as much as I do."

The girls both entered the pretty boudoir where old Lady Marian Dixie was waiting for them. She drew Brenda close to her and kissed her. Then she looked at Florence.

"Why, I have heard all about that young man," she said, "and the week is up; it was up yesterday. Is everything settled? Are you engaged to him? He has stood the test, has he?"

Poor Florence! The tears trembled in her eyes.

"No," she said, "no. Oh, tell her, Brenda, tell her. I can't, I can't!"

Florence walked to the window and looked out. Brenda said something in a low tone to Lady Marian. After a very short time Florence came back. Her cheeks were bright, and so were her eyes.

"I wouldn't have him now," she said, "if—if he were to go on his knees to me—as the saying is. I wouldn't have him at any price. I don't suppose I really loved him."

"It was a good thing you found it out in time," said Lady Marian. "And besides, Florence, you are a great deal too young to marry yet. Why, my dear good child, you are not half educated. Now, my plan for you both is this: that you should go to either Newnham or Girton in the autumn and take a proper course of training there; afterwards, we might go abroad for a bit. In these days, uneducated women are unbearable, and no girl of eighteen, however clever she is, can be properly educated. You can spend your holidays with me, and go and see the Arbuthnots sometimes if you like. But that must be as you please."

"But—but," said Florence in amazement; "of course I'd adore to go to Girton; I have always had the greatest hankering for it. But we can't earn our living in that way."

Lady Marian smiled.

"You don't need to earn your living, my dear child," she said.

"I don't need—Brenda and I don't need! What do you mean, Lady Marian?"

"I mean what I say," answered Lady Marian. "Mr Timmins told you the truth with regard to your father. He unfortunately lost a very large fortune shortly before his death, and could only leave enough by will to be spent on your education. His will was a somewhat extraordinary one. In this, he said that he wished you to be educated to enable you to take your proper position in the world, not only in the world of fashion but also in that better world of refinement and culture: in the world where good people live and valiant efforts are made to maintain the right and suppress the wrong. He wished you to be carefully prepared for this position, for he knew only too well that youth—the early days of youth—is the time for such a preparation. But when you left school (he mentioned the exact age when this was to take place), you were both to be put to the test; and not only you, but your friends. You were to be told the truth, but only a part of the truth. Your father's money, with the exception of a small sum which I believe Mr Timmins mentioned to you, has nearly been exhausted. You were to face the world, prepared in one sense, but unprepared in another. You were to look at the world, for a short time, as poor girls, not as rich ones. Your own characters were to be submitted to this trial and, still more important, the characters of your so-called friends. Do sit down, Florence; how white your face is! Brenda, come and kneel by me, darling." Florence dropped into a chair. Her heart was beating almost to suffocation. Brenda knelt by Lady Marian and looked at her sister with a world of pity in her own eyes.

"You were to find out your friends, my dear children," said Lady Marian;

"and you could only find them out through this test. The girl who has money is often surrounded by so-called friends, who see much in her because her gold casts a sort of false halo round her. Your father wanted you to learn a lesson, so that you could, all through your future years, discern the true from the false. As to the length of the test to which you were to be submitted, that was left altogether to Mr Timmins' and to my discrimination; for I, my dear children, by your father's and mother's will, am appointed your guardian, and have now absolute power to arrange for your future."

"Still—still," said Brenda, speaking with hesitation, "I cannot see where the money comes in. Not that we want it," she continued; "for we have found—oh! such a true friend in you, and Mr Timmins is good—"

"And the Arbuthnots," said Florence suddenly; "they are just more than splendid!"

"And we don't mind a bit earning our own living," said Brenda.

Lady Marian bent forward and kissed Brenda on her brow.

"I know that quite well, my darling," she said; "and I know also that Florence has learnt her lesson. You have discovered your true friends, and also discovered your false ones. What about Mrs Fortescue? What about—" here she glanced at Florence.

"I know, I know," said Florence. "I thought Michael was—oh! so different; and I—I did care for him a little!"

Tears rose to her eyes. She pressed her handkerchief to them and sat still for a minute, trying to recover from her emotions; then she continued—

"I have not broken my heart."

She looked up with a smile which was half piteous.

"I know that," said Lady Marian, briskly, "and you will recover it altogether soon. Now the facto of the case are these. Your father wished his money to be spent on your education. Meanwhile, your mother's money, which represented a very large sum—many thousands of pounds: I cannot go into full particulars, but Mr Timmins will, if necessary, enlighten you—was to lie at compound interest awaiting the moment when you were to receive it. My dear girls, a certain portion of that money is to be devoted to what may be called your *higher* education—that which you will receive during the next three years—and afterwards you will be rich, dears, I trust; not only rich in money, but rich in the better things, which mean courage, and endurance, and faith, and sympathy. You will understand the real poor a little better because for a short week of your lives you considered yourselves poor, and you will discern the true from the false also because of this week, which has taught you a lesson. Now go up to your rooms, dears; I think I have explained all that is necessary for the present."

"But one thing," said Florence, as they rose. "May I write and tell Susie Arbuthnot?"

"Certainly; I should like you to do so."

Chapter Fourteen.

Mrs Fortescue Receives a Shock.

At Langdale, several people missed Florence and Brenda Heathcote. Susie and her father missed them most, because they were the sort of people who would love the girls for themselves, and not for the money they had been supposed to possess. But there were others who missed them in different degrees and according to their different characters. Bridget, for instance, was extremely sulky when she found that Mrs Fortescue had let Miss Florence go without even one word of farewell, nor one allusion to the sorrow she ought to feel at giving her up. Mrs Fortescue herself had her qualms of conscience. The advertisements she had put into the papers were not receiving satisfactory replies. The ladies, old or young, who suggested residing with Mrs Fortescue offered comparatively small sums for the privilege of dwelling under her roof. Mrs Fortescue felt almost snappish. She did not think that she would make much solid gold out of the young ladies whom she was hoping to have to reside with her. She began to murmur at the dispensations of Providence, and to think it cruelly hard on Brenda and Florence that they should be deprived of their fortunes. She began for the first time to see matters from the girls' point of view. It would, in short, be difficult, almost impossible, for her to find any other pair of girls so nice as these, and so well able to pay her for the great trouble she had taken on their account.

She even did not like to think of that morning when she had insisted on depriving Florence of her poached eggs, and giving her a breakfast which under ordinary circumstances would have been partaken of by Bridget. She was also much annoyed at Bridget's determination to leave her; for Bridget was a cheap, as well as a valuable servant; and Mrs Fortescue knew well that such people were rare.

She therefore, when she went into the street, had on an injured and melancholy air, and spoke with sadness about the poor *dear* Heathcotes, wondering what the sweet girls would now do with themselves, and how the cold world would receive these dear orphans, who were so unfitted to plunge into its stormy waves.

One of the people she met, as she walked down the street a couple of days after Florence had left Langdale, was Major Reid. Major Reid felt about as cross as man could feel. He had been worked up to a state of intense excitement during his last memorable interview with Mrs Fortescue. He had hoped great things not only for his son, but for himself, after he had heard what in all probability Florence's fortune would be. He had returned home in a genial mood, and in consequence he and the Lieutenant had engaged that evening in a very amicable conversation. Michael found his father much more approachable on certain subjects than he had ever found him before, and in a fit of confidence he had acquainted his parent with part of the truth, but not all, with regard to his financial difficulties.

The Major swore a good deal when he discovered that his son was hopelessly in debt. Nevertheless, he cooled down after a time, and said that although it would be almost an impossibility, he would endeavour to raise a few hundred pounds to set Michael straight—in short, to put him on his legs again, provided he secured that dazzling young heiress, Florence Heathcote. But now—alack and alas! the dazzling young heiress did not exist. The girl herself was there, with her bright eyes and radiant face and all the fine qualities which the Major had given her credit for. But the glitter of gold no longer surrounded her, and she was therefore an impossible mate for Michael. The Major was choking with rage. Things were much worse than they had been at the Moat, for now the Major and the Lieutenant were scarcely on speaking terms, the Major furiously declaring that he would not advance a penny to help his son, and the son threatening all sorts of disastrous consequences in the future.

Eventually, Lieutenant Reid left Langdale, intending to visit certain money-lenders who, he trusted, would help him temporarily out of his difficulties.

After he had gone, Major Reid cooled down a little. The boy was his only son: he had hoped to see him a useful and popular member of society—a country gentleman, no less; for surely if Florence was as well off as Mrs Fortescue had given him to understand, the boy need not continue in the Army.

All these dreams had now come to an end, and the Major felt that there were few women in the world he hated as he did Mrs Fortescue. He would have given a great deal not to meet her, but he suddenly found himself face to face with her in the little High Street. She came up to him sorrowfully. She was the sort of woman who could never, under any circumstances, imagine herself *de trop*, and she certainly believed herself to be irresistible to all men.

"Ah, Major!" she said. "What a blow—what a terrible blow we have received! and where is your dear boy? I pity him from my heart."

"My son has left Langdale," said the Major freezingly. "I will not detain you any longer, Mrs Fortescue. I am going for a brisk walk, and the morning is too chilly to stand still long in the street."

He raised his hat and walked on. He looked very stiff and disagreeable.

"Old curmudgeon!" whispered Mrs Fortescue under her breath. "What a selfish person! he has no thought for the poor girls themselves; or for me, or for any one but just himself and that conceited puppy, Michael." Mrs Fortescue continued her morning shopping, and eventually found herself in the neighbourhood of the Grange. Surely there, at least, she would receive all possible sympathy. When had Susie turned an unwilling ear to any one's grief? She—Mrs Fortescue—would show herself this morning in the most amiable light, suffering with the penniless girls and not thinking of herself at all. It would be very forgiving of her, too, to call at the Arbuthnots' after the Colonel's visit to her. It would show, that she at least bore no ill-will to any human being on earth.

Accordingly, she paused before the well-known door. She would be obliged to ask Colonel Arbuthnot before long for a reference, and would like to smooth the way by means of an interview with Susie first.

When the servant answered her summons she inquired, therefore, if Miss Arbuthnot was within. She was replied to in the affirmative, and was shown into the parlour looking out on the street. There Susie was performing all kinds of useful arts. It was not at all a pretty room—as pretty rooms go: it was made for use, not for ornament. The table in the centre was an old deal one—in fact, nothing better than a large kitchen table, and at this moment Susie was busy finishing the marmalade which she and Florence had begun.

She looked up when Mrs Fortescue appeared. Her eyes were a little red, as though she had been crying: otherwise, her face was quite cheerful, it even wore a jubilant expression.

"How do you do?" she said in her kind voice. "You will forgive me if I go on cutting my oranges. All this supply of marmalade has to be boiled early to-morrow morning, and the orange peel must soak for a certain time."

"Yes, yes," said Mrs Fortescue; "I quite understand. There are so many recipes for marmalade."

"Mine is the best that is known," said Susie, in her quick voice, cutting her orange peel as she spoke into fine, almost imperceptible wafers. "You don't slake your own marmalade, do you?" she said.

"No; I really haven't time; and that reminds me—Bridget is leaving. It is too bad: she is such a good faithful creature, and I don't know how to replace her."

Susie helped herself to some more orange peel and continued her work.

"You don't know of any one you could recommend, do you, Susie?" said Mrs Fortescue.

"No," said Susie bluntly. "I do not."

Mrs Fortescue heaved a deep sigh. She quite understood what Susie Arbuthnot meant to imply by her brief words. Even if she did know a nice honest girl she would not send her to Mrs Fortescue.

"Susie," said Mrs Fortescue, after a pause, "I fear, I greatly fear that I was a little hard on dear Florence. I have come here to tell you so."

Susie laid down her knife and raised her honest brown eyes to fix them fully on Mrs Fortescue's face. The widow pushed her chair round so that the light should not fall too full on her countenance.

"Yes," she continued, "and I have come here to own my fault. I fear your father was deeply annoyed with me. Is that true?"

"'Annoyed' is not exactly the word," said Susie, in a low tone.

"Well—well, dear," said Mrs Fortescue, who did not wish Susie to say too much and trembled also with regard to her future reference. "You, who have your fixed and settled income can scarcely understand what it is to be a woman of my means—a woman with an uncertain, a fluctuating supply of money; enough just for her bare needs one year, and too little for them the next. I lost my temper—not, indeed, with the girls themselves, but with that exceedingly deceitful man, Mr Timmins, who might have told me how the dear children were placed long, long before he did. He deceived me, he deceived us all."

"The girls were not to blame, were they?" said Susie, resuming the cutting of her orange peel with considerable energy.

"Oh, no, no—indeed no!" said Mrs Fortescue; "and that is just what I have come to talk about. I have recovered my temper and repented of my injustice. I am now thinking, not so much of myself, although I shall have to find some young girls to mother, in the future—"

Susie again looked at her attentively—"but I have not come here to talk of that now. I am anxious about the Heathcotes, poor dears! Poor dears! the world will receive them coldly—"

"I do not think so," said Susie.

Mrs Fortescue shook her head.

"You do not know the world, Susie Arbuthnot. You think you do; but you don't. The fact is—it shudders at the poor, and the older it grows, the more it despises poverty, the more it requires every one whom it takes to its heart to be rich—*rich.*" Susie was silent. "Those poor young things," continued Mrs Fortescue—"if there is any way in which I can help them—I came here this morning. Susie, to tell you that I am willing to do it."

"Are you really?" said Susie. She looked at her abruptly. "Would you, for instance, give them a home if they required it?"

"I—" said Mrs Fortescue, hesitating—"well, not for long—but just for a little visit perhaps. What I really meant to say was that I could furnish them with excellent references, and—what is the matter, Susie?"

"Nothing," said Susie, rising. "I am going to find father. I think he is in the house."

She abruptly left the room, closing the door after her.

"What a very queer look Susie Arbuthnot has on her face!" thought Mrs Fortescue. "I wonder if those people have made up their minds to shun me. If so, and if Major Reid means to continue to be as abominable as he has been this morning, I had better leave Langdale."

As the last thought flashed through her mind Susie returned with the Colonel. They came in together, and the Colonel held a letter in his hand. He was somewhat shabby in his dress. He always was shabby in the house; but he never stooped in body, being a soldier; and he never stooped in mind, being a gentleman. He came forward quite simply, and held out his hand to Mrs Fortescue.

"How do you do? It is a beautiful day, is it not?"

Mrs Fortescue felt immensely relieved. The Colonel had evidently quite forgiven her. He was a nice man and—yes, she acknowledged it to herself—such a gentleman. Susie was very blunt; but the Colonel had exquisite manners when he liked, and he seemed to like now, for he invited Mrs Fortescue to take a warm seat near the fire and poked it up for her benefit. Then, turning his own back to it, he looked at her with a whimsical expression on his pleasant face.

"Susie tells me that you have been good enough to express regret with regard to Brenda and Florence Heathcote."

"Oh, yes—yes!" said Mrs Fortescue, clasping her hands. "I am so sorry for them."

"Well, there is no possible reason why you should not be relieved of any feeling of uneasiness with regard to my two young friends. Florence did not wish her letter to be kept a secret, did she, Susie?"

"No, father; quite the contrary," said Susie. She had not returned to her marmalade. She was standing not far from her father, one of her hands resting on the mantelpiece.

"I have had a letter from Florence Heathcote this morning," said the Colonel. "It was really written both to my daughter and myself."

"Has she found employment?" asked Mrs Fortescue.

"Well—yes; that is, her future plans and those of her sister are practically arranged for the next few years."

"I am very glad," said Mrs Fortescue, speaking in a cold, disappointed voice.

"Ah, well," said the Colonel, "and so am I—very glad. But you haven't heard all yet. You don't know, far instance, what the girls mean to do."

"I do not," said Mrs Fortescue; "and I am so much interested in them— so very much—dear children, dear children!"

"You had an opportunity of showing your interest a week ago," said the Colonel, very gravely—"your interest and your sympathy. The fact is, Mrs Fortescue, both that interest and sympathy have come now rather late in the day—in short, they are not required. The girls go to Girton in the autumn, and until that time, they will be preparing for their life there, under the best masters that London can provide. They will live, until they go to Girton, with Lady Marian Dixie."

"Then she has taken them up!" said Mrs Fortescue, quivering rage in her voice. "She has in a sort of way adopted them? Yes," she continued, half-choking with futile anger; "but they need not trust to the whims of rich women. She may change her mind a thousand times and leave all her money in the end to some one else. I have seen it done—I have known it done times out of number."

"Yes; quite so," said the Colonel; "quite so. In this case the matter is different."

"Has she already made a will in their favour?" inquired Mrs Fortescue.

"I don't know anything whatever with regard to Lady Marian's intentions," said the Colonel, speaking less affably and flashing his eyes sternly at the widow. "The fact is this—you will be as surprised as Susie and I were and, I hope and trust, for the sake of your better nature—as glad. Brenda and Florence Heathcote have no need to earn their bread."

"No need? Oh!" said Mrs Fortescue. "But I was told they were penniless."

"You received a letter from Mr Timmins in which he informed you that the money their father had left for their education was practically exhausted, and that your services would not be required after their winter vacation."

"I was given to understand that they were penniless girls. What do you mean?" said Mrs Fortescue.

"You will be glad to hear that they are very far from penniless. Their mother has left them a large fortune which they will come into as soon as they attain their majority. Meanwhile, Lady Marian Dixie is appointed their guardian. She wishes them to continue their education, and they are going to Girton for the purpose. It is good news—yes, it is very good news. Florence and Brenda will, I make no doubt, be fitted to bear the awful responsibility of wealth."

"But—but," said Mrs Fortescue, almost blue with rage; "how can you justify—"

"I justify nothing, my dear madam; I simply state a fact; you are welcome to tell it to whom you please. As far as I can make out, the girls were not told anything absolutely untrue. As far as their father's money was concerned, they were penniless. There was no mention made of their mother's fortune. It was, I gathered, a test to discover who were their true friends. Rich young girls are often surrounded by those who simply prey on them for the sake of what they can get. Susie, don't you think we had better come out while the sun shines? You won't think me rude, Mrs Fortescue, if I ask you to call at some future date."

"Oh no; I won't think you rude," said Mrs Fortescue. "I—I am astonished—stunned—"

But she spoke to empty air, for Susie and her father had left the room. "They did not even show me out!" thought the furious widow. "Langdale won't see *me* long!"

Perhaps very few people suffered more exquisite torture than did Mrs Fortescue after she left Colonel Arbuthnot's house. Oh! if only she had been good to Florence during that week. Oh! if only she had done just —just what she had not done! She was like many another unfortunate man or woman in this world which contains so many failures! She had acted in the worst possible way at the crucial moment. She had missed her chance. The girls were rich after all, and yet she had given Florence a ham bone for breakfast! She walked fast, trying to cool down after the blow which, it is to be feared, Colonel Arbuthnot rather rejoiced in giving her.

Suddenly, an idea came to her. If she was suffering, why should not Major Reid share her tortures? How impertinent he had been to her that morning! But she was right after all—right, not wrong. That silly fool of a Michael—if only he had been true to his heart's instincts— would have won an heiress, and perhaps an heiress to a far greater extent than even Mrs Fortescue's dreams had pictured.

"I will go to see the man. This is really a good story and one worth telling," thought the widow.

She turned in the direction of the Moat. The Moat was a little way outside Langdale, and you had to go up a somewhat steep hill to reach it. It was an old-fashioned house, surrounded by overshadowing trees. Even in summer it was not very bright, and in winter it was a hopelessly damp, deserted-looking place.

Mrs Fortescue marched up the avenue with a determined stride and rang the bell by the front door. It was opened by a slatternly-looking servant. The Major's house was not kept well. In all respects, it was a contrast to the Grange, where the Arbuthnots managed to make every penny do its utmost work. Nobody cared what became of things at the old Moat, and there was hardly a more miserable old man than Major Reid, as he sat now at his lunch table, trying to find something tasty and agreeable in his badly-done chop. Mrs Fortescue, who was feeling so fierce that she would dare anything, followed in the steps of Colonel Arbuthnot and said quickly—"I know your master is in: I must see him at once on important business."

The girl made way for her, and Mrs Fortescue's instinct drew her to the dining-room. She opened the door and burst in.

"I have news—great news for you, Major Reid."

"Madam!" said the Major. He started to his feet. His first furious request to ask this interloper to make herself scarce died on his lips. He looked into her face. She came close to him and looked into his.

"Major," she said; "we have been the victims of a conspiracy—yes, of a base, base conspiracy. It is my opinion that the Arbuthnots were in the secret from the first, and that hat accounts for their sneaking, fawning ways. How I do loathe people of that sort. So different from you and me—so, so different!"

"You astonish me," began the Major. "The Arbuthnots—pray take a seat—"

He pushed his plate away from him and looked hard at his visitor.

"You were abominably rude to me in the street a couple of hours ago," said Mrs Fortescue.

"I was in no mood to be civil, and even now, if you have anything to say except to abuse my old friend Arbuthnot, I—"

"But I have something to say; something that will astound—*astound* you! When you came to my house a very short time ago and asked me to give you some idea of the extent of Florence Heathcote's fortune, I told you—"

"A lie, madam! The girl is penniless: pray don't revert to that most annoying scene."

"I told you no lie, Major Reid."

"What?"

"I told you the truth. I doubtless understated the sum which will eventually belong to Florence Heathcote."

"What is this?" said the Major, turning very pale.

"The conspiracy has been at last explained," said Mrs Fortescue, "and my opinion is that those Arbuthnots, who set up such lofty standards, knew all about the matter from the first. Those miserable girls are heiresses, after all. Their father's fortune, it is true, has been already expended on their education, but they inherit a large sum—doubtless many thousands—from their mother. It seems, Major Reid, that for some extraordinary, unfathomable reason we, their old and trusty friends, were to be put to the test—to the test with regard to their future: and I—*I* treated Florence, that beautiful, gifted spirited, *rich* girl, to—a ham bone!"

Angry tears rose to Mrs Fortescue's eyes. The Major looked at her with a face very nearly as pale as her own.

"Are you certain of what you are saying?"

"I am positive. I have been to the Arbuthnots'. I received the news from the Colonel himself. He had a letter from Florence in his hand. He spoke of it as a test—a test; but I call it the vilest of all conspiracies! I could still have had those girls with me, and your son would have married Florence and been rich."

"Good Heavens!" said the Major. "If I thought—but it isn't too late. Michael—that young dog! Mrs Fortescue; don't say a word; don't breathe anything. Keep my secret and I vow I will help you in the future. I will go to London to see Michael this evening. All is not lost."

The Major, trembling exceedingly, crossed the room. He rang the bell and desired the servant to bring him an A B C. He looked up a train in Mrs Fortescue's presence. She was no longer hateful to him. If she could help him at this juncture, he would be her friend for the rest of her life.

"Never mind the Arbuthnots," he said. "Yes; they doubtless did know. Just like the Colonel. It *is* a conspiracy—it is shameful! But let me make an effort in my poor boy's cause. Don't breathe to any one that I have gone to London. I will just walk in the direction of the station, and slip in when no one is observing, and take the next train to town."

"I will keep your secret, trust me," said Mrs Fortescue.

Chapter Fifteen.

Turning over a New Leaf.

The Major arrived in town towards evening.

He knew where his son was lodging. Lieutenant Reid would have to join his regiment in two or three days, but the last few hours of his leave would be spent in his old rooms in St. James' Street.

Reid was heavily in debt—up to his very eyes, in fact—but that was no reason whatever for his taking poor rooms or allowing himself to be in the least uncomfortable. He had a very little money in hand, which he had extorted from a rascally old Jew at enormous interest, and was therefore, as he called it, rather flush, and inclined to make the best of things. He was about to go out to dine at a certain club where he would meet some of his brother officers when the Major walked in. It is sad to have to relate that Lieutenant Reid was by no means glad to see his father.

"Why, dad!" he said; "whatever has brought you up to town? and how queer you look and in the name of fortune, what is the matter?"

"I have had the most astounding news," said the Major. "Let me sit down, I am quite breathless. Michael, where are you going to dine?"

Michael Reid mentioned a fashionable club where he hoped to meet his friend.

"You will not go there; you will stay with me. Send a messenger to Hudson to say you are prevented dining with him this evening."

"But why? I have arranged the matter," said Michael, speaking crossly.

"That does not signify in the least," answered Major Reid. "I want to speak to you, and there is not a moment—let me tell you frankly—not a moment to lose."

Michael looked very hard at his father, and something in the old gentleman's agitation seemed at last to acquaint him with the fact that a matter of importance had occurred. He accordingly rang his bell, and gave the necessary directions with regard to securing a messenger boy to take a note to Captain Hudson. He then scribbled a few lines, delivered the note to the servant, and turned to his father.

"I see you are in the old rooms," said the Major.

"Yes; I always come here when I am in town. Why should I change?"

"They are expensive," said the Major. "How do you mean to pay for them?" Michael Reid turned rather white.

"Sir," he said, "you have decided not to help me in the future, you have therefore forfeited the right to inquire into my financial position. It is nothing to you, surely, how and in what manner I manage to obtain a living."

"You cannot go on in the Army, swamped in debt as you are," said the Major. "It is disreputable, and impossible."

Michael, who had been exceedingly annoyed at his father's visit, now stared at him with a certain defiance. Then he looked at him again, and it seemed to him that there was a meaning under the old gentleman's words. He wondered vaguely if his old father was softening towards him, and if, notwithstanding that unpleasant *fracas* with regard to Florence Heathcote, he would help him after all. Accordingly, he sank into a chair, and gazed at his parent.

"You have something to say; you have not come up to town for nothing?"

"Most assuredly I have not. Michael—be prepared for astounding news."

"What, what?" said the young man, his heart beginning to beat.

"You remember that Heathcote girl."

"Florence?" said Michael. "I shall never forget her."

"Oh, Michael," said the Major; "we have been duped, and we have been fools, all of us! I thought when first I heard the news, that Arbuthnot and Susie were in the conspiracy; but in the train, somehow, I changed my mind. Arbuthnot could not do anything mean, nor could Susie. They were the only people at Langdale who treated Florence Heathcote with equal love and kindness in her supposed poverty as in her supposed riches."

"Well, sir," said Michael; "you yourself were the one who said that I must not consider Florence for a single moment as a suitable wife for me."

"I did—I did, my boy. And oh! my God—how I have repented!"

"But why?" said Michael. "Do you want me, after all, to many a penniless girl? But I; father, I can't see her again! I—I behaved abominably to her—abominably. What is the matter with you, dad? Why do you stare at me? What are you so put out about?"

"Put out—put out!" said the Major. "I—I should think I am put out. If the truth must be known, I feel nearly mad. Why, Michael, my boy, the Heathcotes are heiresses after all—richer, far richer than we ever dared to hope. Michael—what is it?"

Michael Reid started to his feet. He stared for a moment across the room as though he felt inclined to do something desperate: then he sank down in a state almost of collapse. In that instant, there came a vision before him of a radiant young face, of speaking and beautiful eyes, and of words he had said—oh! words he had never meant— never meant at all! He had another vision of that face when he had acted cruelly, brutally—towards the sweetest girl in the world.

"You want to hear particulars?" said the Major. "I will tell them. That horrid woman, Mrs Fortescue, was the first to hear the news. Florence wrote to Colonel Arbuthnot. The facts are simply these. The girls inherit a very considerable fortune from their late mother. It was their father's money which was mostly spent on their education and which was nearly exhausted."

It seemed to Michael Reid that Florence's pathetic face looked at him more and more sorrowfully. The room seemed full of her face, full of her young presence, full of the trust she had once given him, and then of the horror and distress which his conduct had caused her.

"Why have you come all the way to London to tell me this?" he said faintly, turning as he spoke to address his father.

"Because—because," said the Major eagerly, "you are a clever young fellow, Michael, and it may not be too late. You love the girl—you have said so—and the girl loves you. Think what it means Michael: don't lose such a golden chance. Is there any possible way in which you can explain your last interview to Florence, and—and win her back? I can assure you that if such a thing can be done, there is no step that I, on my part, will not take to help you."

It was just at that moment that Michael Reid felt something new and strange stirring within him, something he had *never* in his whole life felt before—a germ, the first germ of true nobility and true manliness. The stirring of this new something was very slight at first—so slight that it seemed to him that he had hardly felt it at all. Nevertheless, the colour of shame did dye his face. He rose from his chair, and said in a choking voice—

"Thank you for coming up, dad. I know you mean well. And now, you must be tired out. Shall we go and have something to eat?"

"But you haven't answered me," said the astonished Major. "You allow the precious moments to fly. My idea is this: I thought it all out carefully in the train. Florence need have no reason to suppose that you know anything about her unexpected change of fortune. You can still approach her, as it were, in her state of poverty. Don't look at me like that, my boy. Men have done such things before. You told her once—"

"Yes, father—yes," interrupted Michael, "I told Florence a very, very short time ago—a few days ago, in fact—that were she as poor as a church mouse it would be all the same to me."

"You told her that, Michael, really?"

"I did—I did!" said the young man; "and if you had only seen how her eyes shone and how she looked at me. She thought then that she was poor—poor as I have described. She believed in me then. I told her a lie, of course."

"Your path is clear," said the Major, becoming so excited that he began to pace up and down the room. "You can easily explain away the impression you unfortunately made upon her on that miserable day. You can tell her that however great her poverty, she is all the world to you. Do it, Michael; do it!"

"You want me to tell her another lie," said Michael Reid.

The Major laid his hand, his shrivelled old hand, on Michael's firm, broad shoulder.

"You are young," he said; "you have the world before you. You have the chance of winning the love of a beautiful and very rich girl. You have got into many difficulties which many other young men in your station have, alas! also plunged themselves in. There is a way out; but there is not an hour to lose. Write to her to-night: beg for an interview. She is with Lady Marian Dixie in Cadogan Place. You can see her in the morning. Speak to her quickly—before she gives you her news. You can retrieve your position: all is not lost. No one knows at Langdale, with the exception of Mrs Fortescue, that I have come up to town; no one shall know. I will take the evening train and creep back to the Moat under shadow of the darkness. You cannot possibly have heard the news—so people will say. Act on my advice, Michael—act on my advice."

"Come out and have something to eat," was Michael Reid's response.

And now he took his father by the arm and drew him down stairs, and took him to a good restaurant not far off.

The old man was full of the most intense excitement. The young man was calm and looked collected and firm. That germ of true manliness was growing bigger. That little flickering flame of real nobility was beginning to warm his hitherto frozen heart.

After the meal was over, the Major again spoke on the subject of Florence.

"I understand exactly what you want me to do," Michael replied. "Don't say another word. Keep your own counsel till you hear from me," and this was all the Major could get out of his son Michael.

But he himself felt that his hurried journey to town had not been thrown away. He was almost sure that Michael's future was secure. He trembled with delight.

"If only it is never, never known that I rushed up to town to acquaint the lad, all will be well," was his last thought as he lay down very late that night to sleep. "Mrs Fortescue won't dare to tell; I'll take precious good care that it is not worth her while. No one else has seen me: it will never be known."

So, while the old man slept, dreaming wonderful dreams with regard to Michael, Michael Reid himself fought with temptation and, to his credit be it pronounced—conquered.

In the course of the next day two letters were received by two different people. They were both in the Lieutenant's well-known handwriting. The Major trembled much when his reached him. He looked at it, almost fearing to open it, but by degrees he calmed down sufficiently to wrest the contents from the envelope, and read Michael's few words. They ran as follows:—

"My dear Father,—
"Thank you for coming to see me, and for opening my eyes. They have been opened very wide. I have had a look at myself: I don't like what I have seen, but there is always such a thing as turning over the proverbial new leaf. I have been a cad in the past; I will make a try for being a gentleman in the future. I can't do what you suggest. Burn this, and try to forget our interview of to-night. I have got into a mess, and I will scramble on to my own legs somehow; but not in that way.
"Good-bye, dad. You will hear from me as soon as I have any

news worth relating.
"Your affectionate son,—
"Michael."

There is no use in describing the Major's rage. It lasted for about an hour. At the end of that time, he burned his son's letter and said to himself that he would try and forget him. But this was not at all easy: on the contrary, for the first time since his birth, the Major truly respected Michael, and in consequence could not get him out of his head.

There was one other letter written that same evening by the young man.

"Florence,—
"I have heard of your great fortune. God bless you. I was never worthy of you. I am going to exchange immediately into foreign service; but before I go, I want to take this opportunity to thank you for teaching me a lesson which to my dying day I shall never forget. I was tried in the fire, and was found unworthy.
"Michael."

Florence cried over this letter. She never showed it to any one. Even Brenda to her dying day never knew that Florence had received it. But although the Major burned his son's letter, Florence put hers away into a secret place where she kept her treasures.

"The letter smooths out *some* of the pain," she whispered to herself; "and I can think of him now without sorrow."

The End.